Richard Carpenter's

ROBIN OF SHERWOOD

THE MEETING PLACE

by Jennifer Ash

Originally published in 2019 by
Chinbeard Books & Spiteful Puppet
in partnership with the
Richard Carpenter Estate
The edition published in 2021
www.spitefulpuppet.com

Layout & adaptation for this edition by
Andrews UK Limited
www.andrewsuk.com

CONTENTS

APRIL

PROLOGUE

The rain pelted against the young man's hood as he wove through the trees. But it wasn't the rain that bothered him. He was used to that; used to being wet and cold from hours in the rain, or scorched by the sun or numbed by frost and snow. Watching, waiting, listening…

Years of living in Sherwood Forest had taught him to ignore even the raindrops that found a way to trickle down the back of his neck when his hood was up, and there should have been no way in.

Moving with a silent speed that came from years of existing outside of the law, Much tugged his cloak tighter across his chest.

Why me, Robin? Why did you pick me?

CHAPTER 1

More concerned with keeping the flights of his arrows dry than with sheltering himself from the mid-April downpour, Much approached the location Robin had suggested as a safe meeting place. Just to the right, off the forest's main path, he'd never have known it was there if he hadn't been expecting to see it.

Two tree trunks, a fraction thinner than those surrounding them, provided a narrow gap just big enough for a person to squeeze between. This gap led into a clearing, no more than six feet in either direction. There was space enough for two people to meet, exchange a brief greeting and goods and go on their away again.

Much's gaze landed on the fallen trunk that spanned its middle; it would provide somewhere to sit if the messenger was running late. But as that same messenger didn't yet know where to find him, he returned to the path.

Walking on a few paces, listening intently for any misplaced sounds, Much spotted an oak wide enough to lean against, out of sight, while he waited.

The sense of injustice the youngest of Robin Hood's men had felt since leaving his friends that morning had grown with every muddy step he'd taken.

'Look after the children, Much. Collect the firewood, Much...' Mocking Robin's voice, he kicked a stone, sending it skittering into the undergrowth. 'Clean the horses, Much. I have a job for you Much...you're a man now, Much. You should have more responsibility, Much.'

Resentment tightened in his chest.

Yeah, right, Robin. What you actually mean is, it be pouring with rain and no one else wants to walk through Sherwood, getting soaked to the skin just to buy apples.

The ground made sucking noises beneath his boots as the rain bounced off the leaves above, sending stray droplets of water trickling down his chin. 'What's so special about Papplewick's apples anyway? What's wrong with Wickham or Calverton apples?'

1

Warming his right hand in the folds of his cloak, Much felt the weight of the money pouch knock against his leg.

Robin must think I's stupid. We could buy an orchard's worth of apples for the money he gave me. And why me? If I'm a man now, then why isn't I guarding the camp or going on watch rather than running around as messenger boy?

As he rested under the canopy of the large oak, Much pictured his fellow outlaws back at their spring camp. They'd be sheltered under the trees, a roaring fire keeping the worst of the damp at bay, while the ever present cooking pot bubbled and glooped beneath the skin roof they'd erected to keep rainwater out of Tuck's cooking.

Little John, Will Scarlet, Marion, Friar Tuck and Robin Hood would be sat together, laughing probably, near their source of heat. Laughing at him maybe, for getting drenched to the bone while they were safe and warm. Even Nasir, who'd been about to take his turn as lookout as Much left, would make sure he observed the track ways of Sherwood from a sheltered position.

'This should be Tuck's job or Marion's or...' Much's discontented mutterings died on his tongue. Clumsy footsteps were approaching from the other direction.

He froze as he heard a boot slide in the mud, followed by a grumbled cursing. Instinct took over and Much dived towards the clearing. Lodged between the slim tree trunks, using the fresh burst of spring leaves to add to his cover, he concentrated on the sounds made by whoever was heading his way.

There was just one set of footsteps. Not soldiers then; they always operated in groups. And none of the local foresters would bother to patrol in this weather.

I wonder if it's the messenger from Papplewick?

Much peeped out of his hiding place, staring as far as he dare along the path and was surprised to see a young woman walking in his direction. Her head was bent against the elements and her was hood up. One hand held her cloak closed across her front, while the other jostled with a rain soaked sack as she struggled to keep it balanced over her shoulder. All Much could see of her face was a dripping strand of plaited red hair which had fallen across a forehead creased in angry concentration.

She looks cross. I 'ope she isn't the one I'm looking for, but I bet she is. That'd be just my luck that would.' Much groaned as he saw her stamp closer to where he was hiding. 'Scarlet should be doing this. He's good with women. I's not sure 'ow he does it, but he only 'as to smile at them as they goes all giggly.*

***

Kate would have rubbed the early morning sleep from her eyes, but her hands were wet and numb with cold as one palm gripped the heavy sack, and the other tried to stop her hood blowing down. Twigs split beneath her boots as she grumpily waded through the forest, wondering how her father could have been so callous as to send her out in such weather.

It had only been two weeks since they'd left their old home near Newark to live in the village of Papplewick, within the bounds of Sherwood Forest. They'd been accepted into the small community with a friendly enough welcome, but her father, as the new chief villager, was already feeling the heavy weight of responsibility.

Since her mother had died, Kate and her father, William, had muddled along. Yet her much loved parent's absence was constantly felt, so when an opportunity to leave their old life arrived, William had seized it; hoping a new beginning in a different part of the county would make the empty days easier to bear. Even though she missed her old friends, Kate had followed her father's wishes like a dutiful daughter. She hadn't banked on him appointing her messengers to the outlaws though.

She'd heard of Robin Hood. Who hadn't? He was the people's hero. Some even claimed he was Herne the Hunter's son. But, here and now, as she passed between the rain whipped trees, about to meet Robin Hood or one of his men, Kate started to wonder how true those stories were. Was she really as safe as her father had claimed? If so, why had he lectured her at least ten times on making sure she was careful?

She muttered under her breath, kicking a stick from her path. 'As if moving away from our home wasn't bad enough… now Father sends me out to meet a dangerous outlaw on my own.'

Mocking her father's voice, she spoke louder with every sodden step. 'I'm head of the village, Kate. It's expected of me, Kate. If we want the outlaw's protection then we must show them trust, Kate! Well, sending your only child out as a sacrificial lamb to a hardened outlawed seems pretty trusting to me. I don't even know where I'm going.'

Even though William had told his daughter that the outlaw would find her and show her where to go, rather than her have to blunder around searching, Kate felt lost. Her father had sent her into a dangerous wilderness where a nightmare could lurk behind every tree, with only a load of fruit to defend herself.

'I bet he don't even like apples!'

Screwing her eyes against the wind, Kate heaved the sack further up her shoulder. Slippery from the rain soaked weight, it instantly slid off her arm again. As she tried to catch it, Kate tripped over an exposed tree root and found herself flying, face first, towards a muddy puddle with no way to break her fall. Crying out in shock and pain, Kate's knees hit the ground with a bruising thump. The sack of apples slumped next to her, splashing icy dirty water up her arms and across her face, adding spots to her natural freckles.

'OWWW... oh, great.' Kate scrabbled to collect the fallen apples, angrily lobbing them back into the sack, as her father's final warnings echoed through her head. *Don't get lost Kate... stick to the path Kate...* 'I suppose if you were here Father, you'd be saying, 'pick up all the apples, Kate...'

Suddenly a shadow cast over her as she crouched over the apples, and Kate let out a cry of alarm. A hooded figure was looming forward, his hand on its way to the nearest apple.

'Hey, these aren't for you!' She shrank back, hugging the sack to her like a shield, stammering, 'who are you?' as the stranger knelt down and held out the apple for her to take.

'I'm Much. Don't worry, I really like apples. Are you alright, Kate?'

'How do you know my name?'

'You was talking to yourself.' Much reached out a hand to pull her to her feet.

After only a brief hesitation, Kate allowed herself to be helped, grateful that her new companion had immediately taken the sack, relieving her of the unwieldy load.

'We should gets under cover.' Much led the way between the trees, adding, 'you should be more careful making all that noise in Sherwood. Soldiers might hear you.' He stood for a second, wondering what Robin or the others would do next. 'Wait here. You stay nice and quiet. No shuffling about nor nothing.'

'Where are you going?' Suddenly more nervous than cross, Kate wrapped her arms around her chest.

'I's gonna make sure you weren't followed.'

'Oh. Okay then.' Kate rubbed some heat back into her hands. Glancing around the contained clearing, bravely ignoring the voice at the back of her head that questioned if she could trust this stranger, Kate asked, 'you won't be long will you?'

'Course not.' Much flashed her a grin before disappearing into the forest.

Kate's anxiety grew as she waited. She'd been so angry with her father that she hadn't considered the danger of being followed by someone who wanted to capture one of Robin Hood's men. She'd thought her father had been fussing. Now, sitting on a fallen branch, already too wet and filthy to worry about getting her cloak dirty, Kate hardly dared breathe as she waited for Much to come back.

Trying to hear him moving about the trees, all Kate could make out was the blustery weather whistling through the branches, trying to rob the trees of their budding leaves before they'd had the chance to unfurl.

'All clear.' Much's honest, round face reappeared as if from nowhere, making Kate jump.

'Are you sure?'

'I's sure.'

Fiddling with the edge of the sack, Kate said, 'The villagers in Papplewick have told me about the soldiers. They told me about what happened to the last head villager and his family. They said a man called Sir Guy of Gisburne came and...' Her voice trailed into thin air.

'He had them killed. Yes, I know. T'was a bad time.' Much closed his eyes, trying to banish one of hundred's unwanted images he'd seen during his life as an outlaw.

They'd come across the scene of slaughter too late to help. Gisburne had rounded on the village with a level of cool-headed planning that he wasn't known for, taking everyone by surprise.

The wife and two young sons of David of Papplewick, the former head villager, had been hauled from their ramshackle home and shot without ceremony. Killed fast. There'd been no warning. No chance to call for help.

The other villagers had run from their homes at the sound of the screams but, surrounded by armed soldiers, they had been helpless to do anything other than witness Sir Guy step forward and stab David in the stomach.

Much would never forget how the people of Papplewick had described the relish on the Sheriff's deputy's face as he'd struck again and again, shouting into the dying man's face that he deserved it. That anyone who consorted with outlaws should expect to be treated like the vermin they mixed with.

That was when Robin had promised not to come into the village again. The risk of being seen, and so bringing a similar horrific fate onto another human being, was too great. Instead he'd arranged a series of carefully selected meeting places. Sheltered, difficult to find, nooks and crannies in the heart of Sherwood where help could be both given and received.

Much had never told his fellow outlaws about the nightmares he had. The terrible dreams that haunted his nights every so often. They always featured the people they hadn't been able to save; parading the distorted faces of those who'd perished simply because the outlaws had tried to help them. He suspected the others had similar dreams. No one talked about them though.

An awkward silence fell as Kate, cradling the sack, her back pressed against a tree on the opposite side of the clearing to Much, watched him uncertainly. Wanting to fill the quiet void, he found himself saying, 'I could teach you to move quiet. If you'd like.'

Kate glanced at him through her wet fringe. 'You could?'

'Yeah. We'd all be dead, Robin, Marion, me and the others; if we couldn't move quiet I mean.'

A smile crossed Kate's face, lighting up her features in a way that took Much by surprise. She looked so different when she smiled. Kate leant forward, her voice keen. 'I've heard about you outlaws. Are the stories true?'

'Yeah. They is true. Mostly… sometimes people gets a bit carried away and adds in stuff we didn't do.'

'Oh.'

Not sure what else to say, but finding he wanted to see his companion smile again, Much pulled out the pouch of money, chinking the silver pieces as he passed it to Kate. 'Payment for the apples.'

Kate weighed the coin bag in her hands, and laughed, 'expensive fruit.'

'Yeah…' All of a sudden Much didn't know where to look. Kate's smile was beginning to confuse him. 'I, umm, I should go back. Robin might need me.'

'Yeah. Right,' Kate flicked her plait over her shoulder. 'I should go too. Father will be worried about me.' Retaking the sack from Kate's outstretched hand, Much mumbled, 'you're brave to come so far into the forest on your own.'

'You're brave all the time.'

'Am I?' Much was unsure how to react until he saw the pride on Kate's face, which made him stand a little taller. 'I mean, I am yes. All the time… So, shall I show you how to be quiet then?'

'Next time. I'd really like that.' Kate surveyed the space between the close set trees, with the fallen trunk across the floor. 'Shall I find you here then? It seems a good place to meet. We could use that trunk as a seat.'

Much lightly kicked the mossy log that straddled half of the clearing. 'Yeah. Right. Here. Yeah…see you next time then…'

CHAPTER 2

The silver coin was dull with use. As Robert de Rainault, Sheriff of Nottingham, held it up to the light he found himself imagining all the hands it had passed through since it was minted. Pulling a face, he dropped the mark, wiping his fingers on his robe. He didn't want to think about all the unwashed peasants who might have touched the money sat in the box before him

He hated that most of the coins were destined to be only temporarily his. King John's patience was running out when it came to the lack of taxes he received from his shire of Nottingham. De Rainault therefore, had begun to take precautions against the day when the King's infamously short temper permanently broke in his direction. Checking his servants were occupied, glad that for once, Sir Guy of Gisburne was not flapping at his heels with his latest grievance, the Sheriff slipped three marks into his pocket.

He only took three. More would be noticed, but a shortfall of three was easy enough to blame on Gisburne's lousy counting skills. Three marks was nothing to the king compared to the loss of the two hundred marks that Robin Hood had so recently deprived him of.

Robin Hood. They'd tried everything - but still something more drastic needed to be done. A way had to be found to stop the outlaw's unspoken, but undeniable, rule over Sherwood. Getting up from his chair, De Rainault went to the window. The boundary of the forest wasn't far away. The man who'd made his life a misery for far too long lived so close. Yet it seemed nothing could stop him and his followers.

'I cut one down and another appears…' The Sheriff grunted, 'the Hooded Man is like one of the weeds that have taken over the castle gardens, suffocating everything that attempts to flourish near it.'

'My lord?'

The Sheriff's eyebrows danced up his forehead, 'where the hell did you come from Gisburne? Don't creep up on me like that.'

Scowling, the Sheriff's deputy looked down at his boots. 'I'll get the servants to bang some nails into the soles so you can hear me coming, my lord.'

'You do that Gisburne.' De Rainault shoved the money box across the table. 'It needs counting. Let's see if you can get five to follow four this time shall we?'

'I've told you before; there is nothing wrong with my ability to count!'

'Really Gisburne? Well there *is* something wrong with your ability to make sure the king's taxes actually get to him in London. '

'My lord, I…'

'I don't want to hear it Gisburne.' The Sheriff pointed imperially at the table. 'That is the last of the villages levy for now. This is to be taken to…' he paused, regarding his companion shrewdly. 'No, I don't think I'll tell you where it's to go until the very last minute.'

'Don't you trust me?

'Of course I don't Gisburne, but that's not the point. Sometimes I swear that wolfshead reads your mind.' He took hold of Guy's chin and titled his head towards the light, 'sometimes I wonder if there's a connection…'

'Don't be ridiculous.' Gisburne spat, adding a hasty, 'my lord,' as an afterthought.

Pushing the sharply Norman countenance away, the Sheriff shrugged. 'Either way, the tax money will be taken to a neutral place prior to being ridden to London. Do you think you can manage a short journey without incident?'

'Assuming you bother to tell me where I'm going when the time comes, then yes.' Biting the inside of his cheek, knowing further comment would be a complete waste of breath, Gisburne sat at the table and pulled a candle closer. Taking a handful of coins, he spread them onto the heavy oak table. 'There's no need to watch me, my lord.'

'There's every need Gisburne. As I've repeatedly mentioned; I have little faith in your ability to count!'

'Then why ask me to do it!' The words came out with hissed venom, 'there are others in this castle, the Captain of the Guard, or your steward, the laundry woman perhaps? But no, that would be no sport would it? Not when you enjoy humiliating me so much.'

'Calm down, Gisburne!'

'Calm down, when you continue to belittle me.' He picked a single coin off the table and thrust it in the Sheriff's direction, 'it's not as if I'd pinch any. A little trust would be…' He stopped, his crimson rage morphing into puzzlement as he lowered the coin closer to the light.

'What is it Gisburne?'

After giving it another turn through his fingers, Guy passed the silver mark to De Rainault. 'This is going to sound ridiculous.'

'You astound me, Gisburne.'

'I've seen this coin before.' He raised his hand to curb the Sheriff's inevitable need to tell him there was only so much money in the world and that most coins looked the same, 'do you see that thin bit along the edge, my lord?'

The Sheriff circled the mark in his fingers, his eyes narrowing. 'I see it.'

'I noticed it last time I sat here.'

'But how do you know that it's the same coin Gisburne? They're used again and again, they get thinner with wear. They get squashed and damaged. Rather like people who make stupid suggestions.'

Ignoring the barb, Gisburne feigned patience. 'What I mean, my lord, is that if this *is* the same coin I noted last time, then it has to have been stolen from us and then given back to the poor. Who we then collected the same coin from a second time.'

'And that's because you are incapable of stopping that blasted outlaw from...' His deputy's calculating grin stopped the Sheriff's blast of frustrated rage before it reached full power. 'You're smiling Gisburne. Either your stomach has relieved itself after eating too much pork last night - in which case, pray open a window - or you've had an idea. The former is more likely.'

Sir Guy was no longer listening. Holding the damaged coin against the table edge, he took a knife from his belt and scored a small incision into its side.

'What the devil are you doing, Gisburne? King John would hang you from the highest tree in the forest if he caught you defacing his coins.'

'I'm laying a trap for Robin Hood, my lord.'

De Rainault took a nearby seat and ripped the coin from his companion's hands. The new scratch was barely visible, but as he turned the disc he could feel the imperfection. 'Tell me about this trap.'

'The coin looks like any other. You'd have to know the blemish was there to find it.'

'And the plan, Gisburne?' The Sheriff was already losing interest. There has been so many plans to capture the outlaws over the years, that he'd become bored of hearing about them.

'We place a tiny nick in a selection of coins and then make sure we get ambushed.'

'I beg your pardon, Gisburne?'

'We make it easy for them, my lord.'

'How much easier does it need to be!?' The Sheriff groaned, realising with a jolt how resigned he'd become to the losses the outlaws caused him. 'Robin Hood isn't exactly challenged by our existence.'

'So we don't try to trap him, or his accursed men, not directly anyway.'

'What are you talking about man?'

'The coins on the table, were they taken from the top of the money chest, my lord?'

De Rainault frowned, 'yes.'

'And which village provided the bag of money you added to the box last, my lord?'

Beginning to see what his deputy was suggesting, the Sheriff developed a dangerous smile of his own: 'Papplewick.'

'Papplewick.' Throwing the coin into the air, Gisburne caught it fast, wrapping it into the middle of his fist. 'It seems that the removal of their head family wasn't a sufficient warning to them about the perils of playing with wanted men.'

'You said you had a plan Gisburne.'

'I need to think, my lord.'

'God preserve us!' De Rainault paced as his deputy flipped the coin over and over in his fingers. 'Think quicker, Gisburne!'

MAY

CHAPTER 3

Much tried to wipe the grin from his face as he sauntered through the trees, but his smile wouldn't shift. He felt oddly light as he walked towards the meeting place. Kate had occupied rather more of his thoughts than he'd admit to. He hoped she'd travel through the forest with more care than she had last month.

As he reached the hidden clearing, Much's nerves took over from his sense of elation. Not even confrontations with the Sheriff of Nottingham made him this anxious. He rubbed his palms down his cloak and stepped through the trees. 'Kate, is you there?'

Jumping up from where she'd been sat on the fallen tree, a beaming Kate thrust a wet sack towards Much. 'Hope you like fish as well as apples?'

Much recoiled with a laugh and a splutter. 'That sack stinks!'

'I know.' Kate wrinkled her nose. 'I've been trying not to breathe in as I walked along. So, do you like fish then?'

'Yeah. Little John goes fishing all the time. We eat lots of fish.' Not sure about adding to their heavy fish diet, Much didn't relish the prospect of hurting his friend's feelings by bringing fish he hadn't caught into the camp. 'I'm not sure John'll like you giving us fish.'

Kate dropped the sack to the side of the clearing. 'Father says it's not about the gift, it's about the exchange of goodwill.'

Immediately reassured, Much found himself grinning again, 'Oh, that's all right then. Little John likes good will…he's not so keen on bad Will, though.'

Kate's happy expression clouded into confusion. 'Oh, father bears you no bad will.'

'No, no,' Much brushed her concern away with a wave of his hand. 'Don't worry. That was just me having fun. Will Scarlet can be good and bad, you see. Good Will. Bad Will.'

'Oh, that's okay then.' Kate giggled as she sat down, patting the space on the tree trunk next to her. 'Sit with me, Much.'

'Alright.' Much sat, leaving as big a gap as possible between them.

'Does you have time to teach me how to be quiet? Father says I'm too noisy and I talk too much and I ask too many questions and… oh, a bit like I am now. Sorry.'

'It's nice.' Much risked a quick glance at her face, before returning his gaze to the forest floor. Over the past four weeks he'd spent more time than was advisable speculating how many freckles decorated Kate's nose. 'I don't mind, I mean… It's okay, if…'

'You alright, Much? You've gone a bit pink.'

The outlaw rubbed a hand over his face, 'yeah. Just 'ot.' He gave a chuckle, 'not like last time we meet. We was soaking.'

'We was! It took two clear days for my cloak to dry out.' Kate pushed the offending garment off her shoulders, revealing a dark brown dress and sensibly rolled up sleeves. Much couldn't help noticing that the freckles dotting her face were accompanied by more decorating her arms as Kate added, 'this time all that's wet is that fish.'

'Shall I show you 'ow to move quiet then?' Much leapt to his feet, the action causing his feet to crash loudly against the forest floor.

Kate giggled. 'Well that wasn't quiet!'

'I 'adn't started yet.'

'Of course not,' Kate gave a shy smile. 'You could show me, or you could tell me what you do for Robin Hood.' She spoke faster now, her voice eager and excited as words tumbled from her lips. 'I've heard he's awfully brave and strong and all the girls is wishing they was Marion and…'

'Is they?'

Much was surprised by how put out he felt until Kate murmured, 'well, not *all* the girls obviously.'

The embarrassed silence that fell between them was only brief, but to Much it felt like a lifetime. Kate had asked him to tell her about his life with Robin, but he seemed to have forgotten everything they'd ever done. Every adventure they'd had, every battle ever fought had evaporated in the presence of his companion's kind eyes and speckled nose.

'Come on, stand up.' Kate got to her feet, 'you's going to show me being quiet like Robin Hood, remember?

Pulling himself together, Much said, 'No, I's going to show you how to be quiet like me. I needs to be more quiet than anyone cos I does most of the watching.'

This did not sound exciting. 'Umm, that's important is it? Watching?'

'*Very* important. If I 'adn't bin watching last week, then the Sheriff would've got all of us.'

Kate's eyes widened. 'Really!? What happened? How were you watching?'

'I'll show you. Come on.' Much held up a hand to keep Kate stood behind him while he peeped out of their hiding place to make sure the coast was clear. A moment later he beckoned her forward. 'See that tree over there?'

'The one with the low hanging branch?'

'Yeah. I was up a tree a bit like that what overlooks the Newark Road while the others got ready to stop this bad man who'd bin robbing travelling villagers.' Much spoke with increased confidence as Kate hung on his every word. 'No one could see me. I waited in quiet 'til I saw 'im coming. Then I did my special bird call that Nasir taught me.'

Kate took hold of Much's arm, sending an instant hit of warmth through his whole body, causing him stand stock still as he experienced a sense of shock he didn't want to lose.

'Can you teach me that too?'

Much shook his head, more to bring himself back to earth than to dismiss Kate's request. 'I would but it takes ages to learn Nasir's bird calls, and if I made it now, and the others heard, they might be thinking we is in trouble, and we ain't.'

Kate twisted her plait through her fingers, looking up at Much through her fringe. 'I'm quite liking it just being us. We don't need them visiting do we?'

'Ummm, yeah. I mean no. Umm...'

Sensing Much's uncertainty, Kate urged, 'we could do some of that being quiet training though. I bet it's hard to climb a tree all quiet.'

'Yeah. And it's important too. Pay attention and listen careful; I won't make any noise.'

As he climbed the tree, Much felt the absence of Kate's hand on his arm threaten to curb his concentration as he dodged the leaves with less than his usual practised care.

Watching as he climbed, Kate gasped in surprise as the outlaw blurred from sight. 'You've totally disappeared.' Wandering around the base of the tree, Kate peered into the sky. 'Much? You are still there, aren't you?'

Laughing, Much stuck his head out through the branches. 'Course I is. Mind yourself, I's coming down.' Scrambling down the first few feet, he smartly jumped to the floor. 'See.'

'That was amazing. Can I have a go?'

'Okay... come on then.'

CHAPTER 4

'Stop grumbling Gisburne.' The Sheriff rolled his eyes as he watched the specially selected group of soldiers gather in the castle courtyard. 'If we'd acted on your idea last month then we'd have had to delay the collection of the real tax money and King John would have been even angrier with us.'

'And what happened?' Gisburne glowered as he remembered how the outlaws had appeared as if from nowhere and escaped with over half of the takings before his men had finally fought them off. 'Hood still got most of it, my lord.'

'And whose fault was that?'

Not wanting to go down that road again, Gisburne barked at his men. 'Get that cart loaded, I'm ready to leave.'

De Rainault sighed with deliberate drama, mumbling so the soldiers wouldn't hear. 'Despite all logical reason, you've come up with a plan that might actually work Gisburne. And yet I find myself picturing you messing it up. I can't think why.'

'I won't, my lord.'

'Umm, let's see shall we.' The Sheriff leant back against the wall, regarding the men-at-arms picked for the mission. Each had a well deserved reputation for being next to useless. 'Now you want to be ambushed by Robin Hood, I suspect you'll somehow manage to avoid him completely.'

***

'Much!' Robin shook his friend by the shoulder, 'didn't you hear Nasir's signal? Come on!'

'Eh? Oh, right, sorry.' Much hastily scrabbled to his feet and followed in Robin's wake as they crept nearer to Albury Bridge. Darting his eyes between the forest and the road ahead, Much didn't want to look at the other outlaws in case they'd noticed he hadn't been concentrating. Guilt nudged at Much's

16

conscience. What if they'd been attacked by soldiers while his attention had been elsewhere? What if his daydreaming about Kate had cost one of his friends their life?

Sweat broke out on Much's forehead as he nocked an arrow to his bow. He could hear the cart now. The low grumble of age rutted wheels was accompanied by the march of horse's hooves.

'Only five.' Scarlet's whisper held a frown. 'Why only five? And where's Gisburne?'

'Maybe the Sheriff is tired of losing men,' Little John murmured back.

Apprehension hung in the air as they waited for the cart to brow the curve of the bridge. As their quarry got closer, Much visualised himself handing the tax money they were about to retrieve, to Kate the next time he saw her. Two seconds later the first of the horses passed into plain sight, knocking all thoughts of Papplewick from his mind.

'Now!'

Robin's bow fired as he gave the order. This first arrow, a warning shot, rammed itself into the front of the wagon, landing only inches above the head of the terrified driver.

A second arrow hit the side of the cart as Marion loosed her bow. The others, bowstrings taut, their senses honed for signs of sudden movement, stood at regular intervals across the road, surrounding the cart.

Robin called out at the top of voice. 'Leave the cart and return to Nottingham. We don't want to shoot anyone. But we will if we have to.'

An uneasy hesitation hung in the air. Every soldier looked at his neighbour, their expressions furrowed and confused. It was clear they were more afraid of making a decision that their master wouldn't approve of, than the prospect of dying at the end of an arrow.

'Hurry up and scarper. My arm's getting tired!' Impatient as ever, Will Scarlet yelled across the bridge as he let his arrow fly.

Grazing the arm of the nearest guard, a huge man with a badly scared face, Will's arrow flew on, piercing the wagon with a reverberating thud.

Overriding the howl of the wounded man, an imperious and familiar voice bellowed from the far side of the bridge. 'Retreat! Leave the cart.'

'Gisburne!' Robin launched an arrow in the direction of the order, careful to make sure it wouldn't hit its target. 'I didn't have you down as spineless, Guy. It's not like you to lurk behind your men. Cowardice is De Rainault's tactic, not yours.'

There was no reply as the soldiers, relief plastered all over their faces, circled their horses and galloped back the way they'd come. Only the carter remained, his whole body shaking, his hands gripping the reigns as if they alone were keeping him alive.

Glaring at him, Scarlett waved the end of his bow towards Nottingham. 'Go!' And the carter leapt to the ground and fled across the bridge almost as fast as the horses had.

***

Will and John were still chuckling as they reached the camp. 'Easiest ambush yet! Looks like we're finally getting under Gisburne's skin, the miserable dolt. What do you think Robin?'

Unloading the single small money box from the cart with Tuck, Robin ran his hands through the coins. 'I think that the Sheriff is learning. There's usually twice this amount.'

Nasir inclined his head. 'Maybe he uses two routes instead of one now?'

'Maybe.' Robin felt his palms prickle. 'Something isn't right.'

'Perhaps Nasir's right. The Sheriff must be desperate to get at least some of the tax money to the king.' Marion took hold of the carter's abandoned horse. 'He knows we can't be in two places at once.'

'Perhaps.'

JUNE

CHAPTER 5

The early summer sky was a startlingly clear blue as Much sat on the fallen tree trunk. He knew he was early.

Little John had teased him about setting off before he needed to, but Much wasn't sure why. He had deliberately avoided talking about Kate, beyond reporting that the goodwill gift and money had been exchanged.

Keeping Kate private from the others however, hadn't stopped her occupying Much's mind more than anything or anyone else. The hours between today and their previous meeting in May had felt long and empty. That morning, even as Robin had repeated the message he wanted Kate to deliver to her father, only half of his brain had been paying attention. His thoughts had been caught between the memory of their previous conversations and pondering what he and Kate might talk about next. He wanted to know everything about her. Absolutely everything.

Contemplating the cloudless sky, listening out for Kate's carefree footfall, Much wondered if she'd touch his arm again. Soon he heard the faintest of footsteps and grinned. She was trying to be quiet for him.

Emerging through the trees, Kate glowed with joy. 'Did you hear me coming? I've been practising being quiet all month.'

Much found his arms itching to hold her. Digging his hands into his tunic pockets instead, he laughed. 'Only a tiny little bit and only cos I is *really* good at listening.'

'That's cos of all the watching you do to keep the others safe.' Kate dropped the sack she'd been carrying to the floor. 'It's much lighter this month, thank goodness.'

'What is it? It don't smell like fish.'

'It's erbs.'

'We got 'erbs already.'

'Must be more goodwill then,' Kate shrugged.

'That's nice.' Much patted the trunk next to him so Kate would sit down. 'I got a message for your father. You listening?'

Sitting with her hands on her knees, her face close to his so she could hear every word, Kate nodded solemnly. 'I bin practising listening all month too.'

Much lowered his voice. 'Robin says the Sheriff is sending Gisburne on a tour of Sherwood's villages soon. Hunting for us, I suppose.'

Kate replied with solid certainty. 'They won't find you.'

'No, they won't. We's too clever for 'um.' Thinking better of being too sure of himself, Much added, 'but only cos we is always careful. We've lost people along the way. It's not always alright.' He paused and glanced up at Kate's face. Immediately he found himself trying not to count how many freckles sat on her nose again. 'You will be careful too, won't you?'

'Course I will.' Kate wiped his concerns aside with a flap of her hand before asking, 'what is Robin Hood like? The villagers say he's an Earl's son. That can't be true, can it?'

Much grinned, remembering how difficult the outlaw's had found it to accept that a man with such a privileged background would want to help the poor by donning the mantle of the Hooded Man. He'd never forget the day he'd first seen Robert of Huntingdon. He'd been working as a shepherd in Hathersage, with Little John. They'd been content enough, but their past life in Sherwood with Robin of Loxley had hung over them like a shadow and, now he thought about it, Much couldn't recall them laughing during that whole year. Then, from out of the blue, Friar Tuck had arrived with a stranger. A stranger calling himself Herne's Son.

'It's true. He's the Earl of Huntington's son.'

'Fancy me having a friend who is working with someone so important.' Kate paused, shyly fiddling with the edge of the sack. 'I is your friend, isn't I Much?'

The young outlaw's face blazed as red as a strawberry as he caught Kate's eye. Looking away again, his words dashed off his tongue in a self-conscious rush. 'Yeah. Course, ummm… I's got to go… we're going to Wickham later to sort out.., something. Here's your coins.'

Dropping the monthly money bag at a surprised Kate's feet, he picked up the sack of herbs. 'See you in July. Don't forget the message for your father…'

Much was running by the time he reached the track that led back to the camp. By the time he'd got to the outskirts of their hideout he was cursing himself to high heaven.

Why did I run away? I've been looking forward to seeing Kate all month. I was going to ask her about her growin' up and her friends, and what she does the rest of the month and what her favourite food is and all sorts of stuff.

Furious with himself, Much stamped towards the blaze Friar Tuck was poking into life.

'You alright, Much?' Tuck exchanged a glance with Little John, as their young friend flopped down with an undignified grunt.

'Yeah.' He threw the sack in Tuck's direction. 'You got 'erbs.'

'Very useful I'm sure.' Tuck opened the sack, nodding approvingly.

Looking up from where he'd been sorting out a flight of arrows, Robin asked, 'did you deliver the message, Much?'

'Of course I did! I always does what you ask me to do, don't I!'

'Good.' With an enquiring look in Much's direction, Robin asked, 'anyone heard where and when the next tax wagon in due to pass this way?'

A general shaking of the heads and shrugging followed, as Robin mused, 'it won't be long now. I think we'd better assume that Nasir was right and that the Sheriff is now sending his tax money out in two different directions. We'd better keep an ear out for any rumours concerning what the Sheriff is up to. Yes?'

Murmurs of agreement floated across the camp, followed by a clipped, 'yes!' from Much's direction.

Raising a hand to Robin to stop him demanding to know why Much was so snappy, Marion gently asked, 'Kate okay is she?'

'She's fine.' Much bit off his reply, before quickly apologising. 'Sorry Marion, I'm a bit tired.'

'Of course you are, Much.' Patting him on the shoulder, she tactfully left him with his thoughts. Then, glaring at the five men sat around the fire, Marion's expression told each and every one of them, with crystal clarity, that teasing Much about Kate would be something they undertook at great personal risk.

CHAPTER 6

'Well?'

'I lost one man. I thought I'd better put on more of a show this time so the outlaws didn't get suspicious.'

The Sheriff's eyebrows rose. 'I believe that is the second time you've thought this year, Gisburne. Perhaps there's hope for you yet.' Ignoring the outrage on his deputy's face, he added, 'Robert of Huntingdon is not a stupid man. We won't be able to do this too often. I'd wager he's already wondering why so little money is travelling through the forest.'

'You're right about that, my lord. Hood made it clear they'd worked out that the taxes were being carried in two wagons.'

'Well he's wrong about that.'

'As we intended him to be. Gisburne gave a sly grin. 'Three of the outlaws weren't there. Searching for the other cart presumably.'

De Rainault looked smug until Gisburne added, 'I think one more ambush will be enough, my lord.'

'Another one?! I don't want any more of my money defaced. If much of it reaches King John there'll be hell to pay. The odd coin is bound to slip through our fingers, but we can't risk too many going his way. We'll have to replace the marked coins with our own money.' The Sheriff gritted his teeth at the thought of surrendering his carefully pilfered funds. 'But I suppose it will be worth it. The king will reward us handsomely once Huntingdon is caught.'

'It'll take time for this to work, my lord,' Guy grunted. 'I told you before, we're playing a long game here. The money will eventually get back to us once the outlaws have given it back to the villagers; but some of it is bound to be spent first and…'

'I know, I know.' De Rainault grumbled into his wine goblet, 'but short game or long game, it had better work! Because, I'm telling you Gisburne, if too many scored coins reached the crown's treasury, someone will sniff that something's wrong and it won't just be that wolfshead in King John's firing line.'

'I'm doing my best, my lord.'

'Of course you are, Gisburne,' the Sheriff scoffed. 'Talking of which, shouldn't you be dealing with the other part of your master plan?'

'After lunch, my lord.'

De Rainault tutted. 'God forbid justice should interfere with your appetite.'

***

'If this goes on, we aren't going to have enough.' Friar Tuck trickled the money through his fingers.

Little John closed the pouch he'd filled and threw it onto a small heap of similar bags. 'We covered the entire length of the Newark Road. If the rest of the tax money came out of Nottingham today, surely it has to have travelled that way.'

Much poked anxiously at the money pouches. 'Will there be enough for me to take to Kate next month?'

He didn't see Will Scarlet's eyebrows raise as Robin replied, 'every village will get something, but only enough to pay what's owed to the Crown. They'll be nothing extra. No money to live off.'

'Better than nothing.' Tuck snapped shut the empty treasure box and heaved himself to his feet. 'I'll get this evening's supper going.'

Scarlet laughed. 'Always thinking with your stomach Tuck. It's only lunch time.'

'As if stew cooks by magic!' Friar Tuck raised his hands to Heaven in mock despair. 'It seems my brother wants raw meat for his repast, Lord.' He winked at Much, 'what has Scarlet done I wonder, to make him want to eat like a wolf?'

***

'Every village in Sherwood, my lord Gisburne?'

'That's what we'll say.' Sir Guy lowered his voice so that only the Captain of the Guard could hear him. 'In fact we'll only visit Wickham, Calverton and Papplewick.'

The captain gave a bark of laughter which contained no humour whatsoever. 'Robin Hood's closest supporters.'

'Indeed. However, it will do no harm to let all the imbeciles who live within Sherwood's reach think that we are watching them.'

'Quite so, my lord.' Raising a hand towards the men-at-arms waiting for the order to mount their horses, the captain asked, 'where first, my lord Gisburne?'

'Papplewick.'

***

Robin couldn't settle. Every one of his senses told him Gisburne and the Sheriff were up to something, but what? Had the Sheriff worked out a way to outwit them, by sacrificing a portion of the King's money in return for getting the lion's share to where it needed to be?

Rolling onto his side, he looked across at Marion. She was fast asleep, her hair loose around her shoulders, her hand outstretched, resting only inches from his. They'd fallen asleep holding hands, but Robin had not enjoyed more than an hour's rest. Woken by his racing thoughts, his troubled dreams had thrown him back into consciousness. Too much didn't make sense. The lack of money in the carts for one, the small number of guards accompanying those carts, for another.

Rising to his elbows, Robin watched his friends sleep. The fire had burned low, and they'd crowded close together for warmth, their weapons next to their hands, so they could react to an attack even from the depths of slumber.

Lying down again, Robin put his hands behind his head and stared at the tree canopy above. The leaves stirred in the light breeze, dancing against the night sky. As he watched, the branches above blurred, causing him to blink as the leaves morphed from green to orange and spiralled out of control. Robin's head ached and the hairs on the back of his neck stood up as a voice broke through the swirling vision that blocked out even Tuck's snoring.

He wasn't sure if Herne was there, hidden between the thickly placed trees, or if the words were projecting themselves onto his consciousness.

'Nothing easily won is worth the battle. Lay down the bow to find the marks.'

It was over almost as soon as it had begun. Robin's eyes watered as the movement above slowed and the leaves merged back to their natural hue.

Rubbing his temples, Herne's Son gave up on sleep. 'Nothing easily won…' He turned towards the hollow in a nearby tree trunk where the tax money for the villagers was hidden. He'd been right. Something didn't make sense here. 'Easily won?' Gisburne had almost made it easy for them. Was that deliberate, and is so, why?

Robin sighed into the night.

Herne, why must you always speak in riddles?

JULY

CHAPTER 7

William of Papplewick had once been a muscular Goliath of a man, but since the death of his beloved wife, Martha, he'd lost his ever hungry appetite and his preference for the sort of labour that kept the muscles strong. Yet, despite the loose way in which his flesh sagged on his frame, he still cast an imposing figure as he strode along the paths of Sherwood, his shoulders back, his proud head held high.

A brittle tree root snapped beneath his foot. The crack reverberated through the stillness of the morning, sending a flock of birds twittering into the sky.

'Be careful, Father.' Kate warned as she struggled to keep pace with his stride. 'Much says we shouldn't make noise going through the forest. It's dangerous. Foresters or soldiers might hear us.'

William gave his only child a searching look. 'I wish you took as much notice of what I say as you do this outlaw.'

Feeling colour rise in her face, Kate kept walking. 'We is nearly there.'

'I don't think we can be. I can't hear anyone coming yet.'

Kate tried not to feel exasperated. 'Exactly, Father. Much trains the outlaws to be quiet.'

William stifled a bark of laughter. 'Does he, now? Robin Hood must think a lot of him.' He gave his daughter a sideways glance, 'I think you think a lot of him, too, don't you?'

Glad they'd reached the established meeting place, Kate pointed left. 'We're here. This is where we swap the goodwill for the money Much brings for the village.'

William took his daughter gently by the shoulder.

'You didn't answer me, Kate.'

Much had been sat on the fallen trunk since just after dawn. Determined to apologise for his hasty departure last time, he was beginning to wonder if Kate had been so offended by his flight that she wasn't coming, when he heard footsteps. They weren't quiet enough to be Kate's, not after all he'd told her about the importance of being silent.

A forester? He listened intently for the tone of the footfall. There wasn't one, but two pairs of boots heading his way. Grabbing his bow, Much placed an arrow on the nock as he heard the gruff tone of a man's voice saying, 'you didn't answer me, Kate.'

Kate? Much edged forward with his bow still armed, but with the arrow point lowered, and poked his head between the trees.

'Kate, is that you? I heard a man's voice.' Much's eyes landed on a buckled jacket and a thick walking stick which could easily double as a cudgel. 'Oh, hello.'

A large hand stretched forward in greeting. 'You must be Much. Kate has told me all about you. I'm William of Papplewick.'

Shaking the hand of the man he took to be Kate's father, Much muttered, 'oh. Good.'

As the two men stood, weighing each other up, Kate glanced about anxiously. 'Shouldn't we go undercover?'

'Yeah.' Gathering himself together, Much beckoned them inside the hiding place. 'How can I help you, Sir?'

William leant against the nearest tree. 'I wanted to thank Robin for his information. Sir Guy of Gisburne came to the village three days after your warning came. He was… determined.'

Much's forehead creased. 'Did he hurt anyone?'

Kate sat as close to Much as she dare in her father's presence. 'Me.'

'What?! Much jumped up fast, drawing a knife before he'd registered that the threat to Kate wasn't actually there. 'How dare he, I'll…I'll…'

'Much, it's okay.' Kate reached out a hand to steady him, her voice shaky. 'I'm fine. He only shoved me a bit. Ummm, can you put the knife away please?'

'Eh? Oh…sorry,' He sheathed the blade with an embarrassed shrug. 'I was angry, I…I hopes I didn't scare you.'

Kate smiled. 'You could never do that.'

Shrewdly assessing the situation that was clearly developing between the outlaw and his daughter, William spoke fast. 'That's why I'm here. Gisburne frightened us. He frightened my daughter. The last head family in Papplewick… they might still be alive if the village hadn't been helping you and…'

Guessing what her father was about to say, Kate was horrified. 'You can't! Our people need Robin Hood's protection. We need his help to pay the taxes. If Much hadn't warned us Gisburne was coming he might have found the money and…

'But if we hadn't had the money in the first place, then we'd have had nothing to hide and...'

Much bit back a sigh. He had heard this argument so many times, and suddenly he felt bone numbingly weary of it all. Tired of the circle he and his fellow outlaws seemed to go around in. They'd help the locals and try to curb the greed of the Sheriff and his kind, but then the villagers would get scared and turn the outlaws away – right up until they were desperate for food and money to pay what was due. Then they'd ask Robin Hood for help, and the whole cycle would begin again.

Already knowing his appeal would be hopeless, Much tried anyway. 'Why didn't you let us know straight away, we could have...?'

Kate's father was adamant. 'You could have done nothing. Any additional contact with you or your friends would have bought greater danger to our village.'

With more patience than he felt, Much asked, 'you'll have to find another way to pay the Sheriff. How will you do that?'

William acknowledged the point with a curt dip of his head. 'I don't know. But it is my responsibility to keep everyone safe. If Sir Guy or the Sheriff of Nottingham discovered that Kate was meeting you like this every month then God knows what they'd do to my child.'

Kate held his arm. 'Father, I'm fine. Really! It was nothing.'

'No.' Much lowered his eyes to his boots as he spoke so no one saw the bloom of regret that darkened his complexion. 'Your father's right. If anything happened to you, I'd...' He broke off and turned to William. 'Do you want the tax money for this month?'

'Where did it come from?'

'It's probably the same money you had last month. We got it back in an ambush after Gisburne had taken it to Nottingham castle to be counted and then bought it back out again to go to the King.'

Kate's eyes grew wide in wonder. 'An ambush! Did you watch from a tree and wait quiet like until it was time to attack?'

Much nodded, trying not to lose the smile he was bribing his muscles to plaster convincingly across his face.

'Father, they did that for us. They rescued the money for *us*!'

William regarded his daughter thoughtfully. 'So the money is going around in circles. Clever.' Drawing Kate protectively to his side, he came to a decision. 'Thank Robin for me. We are not ungrateful, but we won't be taking any more money.'

Much gaped at Kate. She was returning his air of horror at the idea of their monthly meetings coming to an end.

'But, Father...'

William shook his head. 'Come on, daughter.'

Pulling away, Kate pleaded, 'Father, Much is my friend. I can't just...'

'I said come home, Kate!'

***

Long after Kate had departed, Much sat on the moss covered tree trunk, feeling strangely empty and with his head thumping with frustrated anger. All he could see was Kate, frightened and isolated as Gisburne rode through her village, slamming her to the ground as if she was nothing more than a jousting butt. He had an urge to go to Nottingham rather than back to the camp. He wanted to pinch William of Papplewick's cudgel, storm the castle, and hammer it around Gisburne's face, until the nobleman's ears rang and his stuck-up nose bled.

AUGUST

CHAPTER 8

'She isn't going to come this month. This is silly.'

The money Much had carried with him, just in case Kate defied her father seemed to mock him from within its fabric pouch.

Closing his eyes, Much let the heat of the summer morning soothe his troubled mind. As if his disappointment at not seeing Kate every month wasn't bad enough, when he'd returned to the camp the previous month, with the news of William's decision not take part in their regular exchanges of goodwill anymore, tempers had become frayed. That row however, paled into insignificance compared with last night's outburst after he'd asked Robin for the money to bring to Kate today, just in case she turned up.

Anyone would think it was my fault William changed his mind about having our help.

***

'I've said it before; some villages just ain't worth helping!' Will Scarlet threw his bowl of pork to the ground in disgust. 'We went thru' this last month! When are you gonna get it, Robin? You can't help people that are too scared to be helped!'

Crouched by the fire, his friends' hectoring ringing in his ears, Much's palm tightened around the handle of the knife he'd been sharpening as Robin responded to Scarlet's familiar complaint.

'And when are you going to see that it isn't their fault they're scared, and if we don't help them no one will! If Much wants to go to the meeting place on the off chance, we should let him.' Every inch the earl's son, Robin's voice held a tone that no one would brook an argument with.

No one that is, except Will Scarlet.

'It's all so pointless. We risk our necks for these people again and again and...' Leaping up, Scarlet knocked his food bowl with the toe of his boot, sending it flying into the flames in the process.

'Careful!' Tuck yelled across the fire, 'I spent ages roasting that pig.'

'Alright, Tuck, it was an accident.' Glaring at Much, as if the ruined supper was his fault, Will snarled, 'honestly Much, I'd have thought you'd have learnt 'ow it is by now! The Papplewick folk turned you away last time, how can you even think about going back to the meeting place tomorrow?'

Much didn't think about what he was doing until the knife he held was lodged at an astounded Scarlett's throat and the other outlaw's were on their feet, gathering around him as he seethed through clenched teeth. 'I'm going. She might be there and I's going to take the money. They need it.'

Vaguely aware that everyone was talking at once, telling him to lower the knife and that Will didn't mean it, Much protested, 'you didn't see 'ow pale Kate went! *You* never saw her face when her father told me 'ow Gisburne had scared her.'

'Alright, Much.' Hoping no one had noticed the split second of fearful uncertainty that had flashed through his eyes as his youngest friend attacked him, Scarlet wrapped a palm around Much's weapon hand. 'I'm sorry. You're right, I wasn't there. I didn't see.'

'Right.' As the reality of what he was doing hit Much, he hastily lowered his arm and let the dagger fall to the ground. 'I'm going anyway.'

The assorted expressions of resigned frustration, which had crossed the other outlaws faces while Robin and Will had been arguing, had been replaced with surprised concern. Concern aimed solely in Much's direction.

'Do you want to talk about it Much?' Little John stepped forwards, his arms open.

'No. No thanks John. I wants to be on my own.'

Moving to a clump of trees a few metres from the fire, Much slumped against the foot of a wide trunk, shutting his eyes to the worried faces that watched him go. Soon he could hear Marion and Robin having a private hushed conversation, but he couldn't make out what they were saying because Tuck was boisterously clattering his wooden spoon around the cooking pot. Beyond that, Much could hear the lowered grumbling voices of Will and John.

I bet they be talking about me.

Shocked at himself for pulling a knife on Scarlet, an act that would have been suicidal to anyone outside of their group, Much gulped. He was lucky he wasn't dead.

He wondered what Kate was doing. He hoped she was alright and that her father would let her meet him in the morning. Or, maybe, if not…well…

if they couldn't see each other anymore, then perhaps he could learn to take comfort in the fact that their sacrifice would keep her safe from the attentions of Gisburne and the Sheriff's men.

Some comfort.

The nagging voice which occupied his daytime thoughts, and had been keeping him awake at night, increased in volume. *How will they pay the taxes?* Then, for nowhere, it was nudged away by the memory of Kate's contagious giggle, and he smiled despite himself.

A movement in the leaves to his left made Much lift his head from where was he sat, with arms wrapped around his hunched up knees. A figure watched him from between the trees. 'Hello Marion. I'm sorry I shouted.'

Slipping into full view; a bowl of Tuck's cooking in one hand and an understanding smile on her lips, Marion gestured to the ground. 'May I sit with you?'

Much shrugged.

'I think you should go to the meeting place in the morning.'

Surprised, Much patted the earth next to him. 'What if Will's right?'

'I think Kate will be there even if she can't take the money.'

'You do?'

'At least, I think she'll *try* to be there. It'll depend if her father manages to stop her.'

'How can you say that, you don't know anything about her?'

Marion's smile lit her eyes as she put a comforting arm around Much's shoulders. 'I know she is brave, I know she is kind and I know you care for her.'

Much stuttered as he felt his face colour as scarlet as Will's temper. 'How did you know?'

'Because you just pulled a knife on the most feared man in Sherwood Forest.'

Much rubbed his forehead as if trying to scrub away his tumbling emotions. 'Oh yeah. So I did.'

'You did that for Kate. For her honour. For the villagers of Papplewick who have never, in all the years we've helped them, been anything other than kind and as helpful as they could be.'

'And then Gisburne killed the old head family and...'

'Exactly. They have every reason to be afraid, and not because of you, or even us, but because of the Sheriff's heavy handed rule.' Marion passed Much the plate of food she carried. 'Eat up, get some sleep. If Kate can be there, she will be. If she isn't, it does not mean she didn't want to be.'

'But...'

Marion got back to her feet. 'Trust me.'

***

'What was that?' Much was pulled out of his uneasy memories of the previous evening by the lightest of sounds. A wren had landed on the trunk next to him. 'Oh, hello little bird…Kate isn't coming, is she?'

The bird cocked its head to one side and hopped to the ground.

'I don't know why Marion was so sure she'd be here.' Hoping his friend was right about Kate wanting to be here, even if she hadn't been able to come and meet him, Much talked to the wren as it bobbed about.

'I was glad to get away from the camp this morning. I think Marion must have told the others off, cos this morning Will muttered something that might have been sorry. He hardly ever does that. I wish I hadn't pulled my knife on him though. Every time anyone mentioned Kate or Papplewick over breakfast, John smirked at me. Maybe I'll stay here just a bit longer, in case Kate does make it.' Much tucked the money bag back inside his tunic, his sigh rebounding around the enclosed space. 'Are you going to sing me a song while we wait little bird? I do hope she's alright.'

SEPTEMBER

CHAPTER 9

Kate's belly growled as she sat on the trunk. Cuddled up in her cloak, she felt cold despite the last rays of sunshine from an unseasonably long summer doing their best to pierce the leaves and warm the meeting place.

'Please come, Much.' Kate's guilt at not seeing him last month had dried her throat and was making her head ache. 'Please come and find me.'

Resting her chin on her bent knees, she listened cautiously, aware of every tiny noise in the forest. There had been birds singing a minute a go, but now it was eerily quiet. Wishing she was brave enough to climb a tree without Much, so she could see the pathway that ran past her hiding place, Kate tried to concentrate.

Flinching with every fresh sound, Kate sat up straighter, straining her ears to hear. *Is someone coming?*

A few seconds more and she was in no doubt. She could hear footsteps. 'Much?'

Her brief surge of hope died in her throat as the sound got nearer. Two pairs of heavy, uncaring, boots were heading in her direction. *Soldiers?*

Not daring to risk moving in case she stood on something and gave herself away, Kate put a hand over her mouth to stifle the sound of her breathing. *Don't find me. Please don't find me.*

The men's footfall got louder with each beat of her heart and, just as she thought they were going to burst in and find her, the noise faded as they walked by.

Exhaling slowly, Kate wrapped her arms around her chest. 'Oh, Much, where are you?'

'I's here.' Much dropped from the tree directly above her.

Kate's mouth fell open. She didn't know whether to be relieved that he was there or furious that he hadn't told her that he'd be nearby all along. 'How long have you been up there?'

'Since before you arrived. I was waiting till the danger had passed.'

She shuffled in embarrassment. 'Did you hear me calling you then?'

'Yeah, but only a little bit cos I taught you to be quiet really well.' He sat next to her. 'The soldiers have gone. Sorry I couldn't reassure you before, but I couldn't risk giving you away by calling out. I wouldn't have let them hurt you.'

'Thank you, Much.' Kate couldn't meet his gaze, so self-consciously studied the forest floor instead. 'I wasn't sure you'd turn up, not after what Father said, and after I didn't come last time. I tried to but... I'm sorry. I don't have anything to give you today.'

Warmed by the knowledge that Marion had been right, that Kate had tried to see him last month, Much said, 'you're here now, that's all that matters.' He looked at her properly. She'd lost weight since he'd seen her two months ago and her normally open appearance showed lines of care.

'Does your father know you're here?'

'No.' Kate started to sob. 'Oh, Much, he's been gone ages! We don't know where. He went to Nottingham market and never came back. Everyone keeps talking in whispers about how the last head villager was killed and...'

It took all Much's energy not to hug her as Kate sat with silent helpless tears streaming down her face.

'It's alright. We'll help you.'

'But father turned your help away.'

Much reached out and stroked a hair away from Kate's tear blotched cheek. 'Because he was afraid for you, not because he's against us. Wipe those tears away. If you're going to be a brave outlaw like me then you can't cry.'

Sniffing as she scrubbed at her face with her sleeve, Kate was suddenly eager. 'I could be like you?'

'Yeah. Why not?' Much realised he wanted nothing more than to take her back to the camp. 'You can already move all quiet and listen proper and you're brave to come here. And anyway, I reckon Marion must get fed up being the only girl...' He paused, suddenly not so certain. 'She didn't like Meg staying when John bought her to the camp, though. But Meg can whine a bit.' Much found himself picturing Kate sat next to the camp fire with him and his friends. She was different to Marion and Meg. 'I reckon you'd be safer with me anyway.'

Not sure how she resisted the temptation to throw her arms around his shoulders, Kate stood back and regarded him properly. 'I would love it, but my father...' Although Kate's eyes still shone, their moment of hopeful happiness dissolved as fast as it had arrived in the face of duty. 'He's all I have. I can't leave him. If I can't find him again...'

Embarrassed, Much said, 'Yeah, course…sorry…' as the sound of Kate's stomach rumbling cut through the clearing.

'When did you last eat?'

'Late the day before yesterday. Gisburne took all the food.'

'He did what?!'

'Said we was no better than animals, so we should forage like they do.' Kate pulled at her plait in agitation. 'Then he reminded us that the foresters would be patrolling in case we had ideas about poaching for food in the forest. He said…he said…' she swallowed to free the words which snagged in her throat, 'he said we'd better start looking for another head villager.'

Much's hatred of the Sheriff's lackey rose to new heights as he took an apple from his pocket. 'Here, have this.'

Too hungry to hesitate, Kate crunched her teeth into the fruit, thanking Much through a generous mouthful.

'It's one of the last of the apples you gave us. We hide food in case the winter is hard. So it's your apple anyway.'

Waiting until Kate had finished eating, Much said, 'tell me exactly what happened. Then we'll make a plan and I'll take it to Robin…'

***

Nasir jumped down from his lookout post, landing without a sound by Much's feet as the young outlaw ran through the forest.

'I wishes you wouldn't do that, Nasir, you near scared me to death.'

Not wasting time arguing, the Saracen said, 'You're worried.'

'How did you know?'

'I know your face.' Nasir matched Much's hurried pace. 'The girl. She is in trouble.'

'Yeah.' Much didn't bother asking how Nasir knew that, too. 'I must speak to Robin.'

The arrival of Nasir and Much together bought the other outlaws to their feet.

'What's happened?' Robin came forward, 'Kate?'

Much's words came out in a fountain of concern and frustration. 'William of Papplewick, that's Kate's father, he's gone missing from Nottingham market.'

'Oh great!' Will groaned, raking a hand through his hair. 'Now they'll want our help finding him, I suppose.'

Ignoring Scarlet, Robin hooked his bow over his shoulder. 'When was this?'

'Yesterday. He set off early but never came back.' Much took a mouthful of water from the cup Tuck offered him. 'Not long after William left for the market, Gisburne arrived at the village. He took all their food. I mean everything. He told them they'd better get hunting for a new head villager.'

'Gisburne knew William was going to be taken then.' Marion reached for her cloak and wrapped it around her shoulders. 'We must go to the village. Tuck, is there any food we can spare?'

'Aye, little flower.' Tuck busied himself gathering supplies into a sack.

Watching his friends bustle into activity, Robin reluctantly reminded them, 'after David and his family were murdered, we promised we wouldn't go into Papplewick.'

Much was furious. 'But they're gonna be starving soon Robin.'

Robin put his hand up, 'I didn't say we wouldn't go! We'll have to be very careful getting food in though, Gisburne will probably have men spying on the village.'

Fidgeting as he waited to hear what Robin was going to do about rescuing William, Much added, 'Gisburne told Kate that her father had been taken by the Sheriff because he'd used stolen money to pay the village taxes. He said he could prove it. That's our fault. That is!'

'Prove it?' Robin's brow furrowed, but there was no time to think, for Much was dancing impatiently from one foot to another.

'We have to put this right, we must go now!'

'Go where and do what?' Will stalked in circles around the fire. 'Get the villagers some food, yes; if we can get it to them safely, but then what? We don't even know where William's being held.'

'Probably Nottingham Castle.' Little John leant on his quarter staff as pulled thoughtfully at his beard.

'Well obviously the castle!' Will growled, 'but there ain't no chance we'll get in there again. The Sheriff's a fool, but he ain't stupid.'

'Alright!' Robin turned to Much. 'Kate got out of the village so she could meet you without being seen, so there must be a way in.'

Much nodded as he warned, 'there was soldiers patrolling the path near where we met this morning. Only two, but they was armed with crossbows and swords.'

'Gisburne really *is* learning.' John tapped his staff against the ground. 'Do you know the way Kate got in and out of Papplewick, Much?'

'No, but I reckon I could find a way in.'

Robin placed a hand on Much's shoulder. 'I know you want to help Kate, but I don't think you should be the one to take the food.'

'What? But I...' Much was close to shouting.

'You're the only one who knows what William of Papplewick looks like. I need you here to help me plan how to get Kate's father back.'

'Oh.' Glad that he was at least going to be able to assist the villagers, even if he couldn't risk going to Kate, Much tense shoulders relaxed a fraction. 'Alright then.'

'I can go.' Tuck launched the sack onto his broad shoulder. 'I'll be careful.'

'Okay, see if you can find a way in. But any sign of trouble, come back. They've not been long without food. Better they go a little longer than we have to worry about the prospect of rescuing you from the Sheriff as well.'

Robin got to his feet as he continued to issue instructions, 'Nasir, Much, we're going in search of information. I want to know exactly where William is and how he came to be taken. As soon as we're back and we know where he is, we're going to get him.'

'What about the rest of us, Robin?' Little John was restless and wanted to get moving.

'Sort the weapons and get some food ready for us when we get back. We have a man to save.'

Marion, who'd been watching Robin carefully, reached for his arm and drew him to one side, 'You know something don't you?'

'Suspect something yes.' He checked over his shoulder. Much was waiting impatiently next to a contrastingly serene Nasir. Lowering his voice, Robin shared his concerns with Marion. 'Gisburne told Kate he could prove that we've been helping them, but we've been nowhere near Papplewick. It's made me think about something Herne said a while ago. I assumed it was about the tax money ambushes, but now I'm not so sure…'

CHAPTER 10

Rumour about the disappearance of William of Papplewick had already blown on the summer breeze, skipping through the leaves on the trees and singing in the forest dwellers ears' to the tune of gossip. Robin, Nasir and Much hadn't even walked halfway to Calverton when they picked up the information they'd been hoping to discover.

Scouting ahead of the others, Nasir had encountered three separate groups of villagers on their way to Nottingham market, each of which had told a similar tale. Although the versions of events varied depending on who was asked, for the story had already gathered extra twists and turns as it had journeyed from merchant to customer and beyond, the underlying facts remained the same. William of Papplewick had been taken by the Sheriff's men while buying some curing salt at the market in Nottingham. Protesting his innocence, he'd been surrounded by armed soldiers and corralled towards the castle gates. Several villagers reported people saying they'd heard the Captain of Guard loudly gloating that Papplewick's head villager was being taken into custody on the orders of Sir Guy of Gisburne, for theft and collusion with outlaws.

Robin said nothing about what they'd learned as they'd headed back to camp. The more he considered Herne's warning, the more he was sure it concerned William, but he still couldn't see why.

Nothing easily won is worth the battle. Lay down the bow to find the marks.

Playing the message through his head, Robin frowned He hadn't fought William, nor had he any intension of doing so. But Herne had come to him not long after Gisburne had first threatened Kate at Papplewick…so maybe it was all about making sure they lay down their bows and kept their promise not to go to the village? Robin flicked a stray blonde hair from his eyes and groaned. He was clutching at straws.

Nasir heard the footsteps a few seconds before Robin did. Holding up a hand, the Saracen stopped dead. 'One man. Heavy on his feet.'

Concealing themselves amongst the trees, the three outlaws soon saw a stray traveller. To their surprise he wore the distinctive uniform of the Sheriff of Nottingham.

Robin stared at him suspiciously, muttering, 'I know that man. You see the scars on his face?'

'I have seen him before also.' The dagger Nasir held glistened in the sunshine. 'Look how he sways.'

Much, who thought the lone guard could have been any one of the many uniformed men he'd seen that month, watched his unsteady progress. 'He's drunk isn't he?'

'He is and he could be useful.' Robin studied the figure for a while, then with a quick nod to his friends, stepped out of cover. Pulling his sword as he landed in front of the guard, Robin heard Nasir and Much emerged from the trees behind him, their own weapons drawn.

Speaking as if the blade he held was invisible, Robin's tone was jovial. 'A dangerous game to walk through Sherwood alone in such garb, my friend.'

The soldier came to a semi-standstill, his feet tottering to one side as he struggled not to fall over. 'Life is dangerous, my fine fellow.'

Nasir's eyebrows rose as he exchanged a surprised look with Much at this unusual greeting between outlaw and soldier.

Robin was equally surprised. 'Do you know who I am?'

'Aye, you're the one olé Gisburne is always on about.' He staggered to one side, reaching an arm out to the nearest tree for support while taking a swig from his ale pouch, 'you tis why I'm 'ere.'

The outlaws tensed at this admission as Robin asked, 'You're looking for me?'

'Nah, I be getting away from 'im and 'is obsession with catching you.'

'Gisburne?'

'Trap meat, that's all we is.'

'Bait you mean?'

The man hiccupped, and wiped the resulting unpleasant stream of dribble from the corner of his mouth. 'Not just me. We worthless to likes of 'im.'

Seeing the man was incapable of standing, let alone attacking three armed men, Robin relaxed his sword arm and Nasir swapped his bow for a knife. Much, however, kept a careful aim with his sling.

'Where will you go?' Robin asked.

'Away. I don't care where. Just me to worry about.' He waved vaguely towards the west, 'Wales maybe. I is going while the Sheriff's away and Gisburne's busy playing at being in charge.'

Thinking of William trapped in Nottingham castle, Much asked, 'where's the Sheriff?'

The runaway guard shrugged. He neither knew nor cared who was where, providing he wasn't on the receiving end of their orders.

'Before you go,' Robin gave the guard a friendly pat on the back, 'why don't we have a little chat?' He gestured for Much to pass over the skin of ale he had at his belt. 'A drink between travellers.'

'Most kind.' The soldier plummeted down where he stood, as if his legs were glad of the excuse to give up the unequal struggle of keeping him upright. Hiccupping he threw his drained skin away and glugged heartily at the offered ale.

'So,' Robin gave their guest a dazzling smile, 'what can you tell us about being bait? Anything to do with the movement of tax money?'

'I don't know if I ought to…' The guard felt himself sobering up too quickly for his liking as the Saracen sat next to Robin Hood. The dark man's smile seemed impossibly wide. *Surely his teeth shouldn't be so white?* But it wasn't Nasir's calm grin that captured the guard's attention. It was the knife he was absentmindedly polishing in his slender hands, and the fact that the younger outlaw had stepped forward; hovering a little too close for comfort.

It dawned on the soldier, rather too late in the day, of what the implications of being in the company of such men might be. The fact that two of the outlaws were smiling at him made it feel worse. Only the desire to stay alive stopped him shuffling backwards into the forest. The soldier found himself scratching at his arm as the memory of Will Scarlet's arrow cutting a slice off his flesh, suddenly parked itself in the tiny part of his brain not addled by drink.

Robin gestured from Nasir to Much and back to their companion. 'What do they call you?'

''Arold.'

'Well, Harold, let's try again shall we? What can you tell me about the movement of tax money and Sir Guy of Gisburne's interest in the village of Papplewick?'

Harold gulped, 'well, I um…the…the Sheriff says taxes were going to be mocking 'em.' A guttural burp escaped from Harold's throat as he shook his head. Mocking 'em. That's all he goes on about, apart from money of course. They's both mad for marks and stuff.'

'And?' Robin backed away from Harold a fraction as he gave another acidic burp.

'All I knows is there's gonna be a late winter tax gathering from the people.'
He groaned, 'but I'm all done with being trap-meat. Can I go now?'

'Soon.' Robin smiled. 'Soon. I just have a few more questions.'

***

As they walked back to camp, Much's head crowded with pictures of William
languishing in the pit which operated as Nottingham castle's dungeon. Each
of the scenarios he conjured was worse than the one before. Much shivered.
He'd been there twice and hoped never to see the inside of that cursed place
again. The stench of stale air, rotten cabbage and human waste was only
drowned out by the fear of those trapped within the damp unfeeling stone
as they waited, unsure if there was anything to wait for beyond a trip to the
hangman's rope or the executioner's axe.

Only one way out of here. Feet first.

'You alright, Much?' Robin gave his friend a sideways glance as they
manoeuvred through the trees.

'I keep thinking about William. It's freezing in that dungeon, even in the
summer. He'll be so frightened.'

'I know.' Robin patted Much's shoulder, 'but we're going to get him out, or
rather Gisburne is, and then we're going to get him back to Kate.'

'Gisburne is?'

'Or our friend Harold has been so helpful, it would be a crime not to act
on such generously given information, don't you think?'

CHAPTER 11

'Are you sure about this, Robin?' Marion slid a handful of arrows into her quiver.

'You know Gisburne! He won't be able to resist driving the prison wagon through Papplewick so he can gloat at the villagers.'

Much was confused. 'But why would he be driving William anywhere?'

'Didn't you think it odd that the villagers we met told Nasir the captain was heard shouting that it was Gisburne's orders that had instructed the taking of William and *not* the Sheriff's? Then, when Harold told us that the Sheriff isn't in Nottingham I remembered; De Rainault's holding his Hundred Court in Newark this month.'

'Which means any prisoners that stand accused of a crime need to be taken to Newark to be tried.' Marion's eyes shone with understanding. 'You're right Robin. It's only a mile or two's detour to pass through Papplewick. Guy will never be able to resist the opportunity to intimidate the other villagers by showing off his captive.'

Much hung back from the others. He was dying to ask if any word had come from Tuck, but didn't want John to smirk at him again. Busying himself with gathering up small stones to add to his sling shot pouch, he was relieved when the friar finally tottered into the camp.

On seeing Much, Tuck raised a hand in greeting. 'She's fine, my boy. Hungry and naturally worried about her father but full of hope of a bold rescue from her handsome friend.'

Much blushed as he mumbled his thanks. 'Did you see anyone watching the village?'

'Just two soldiers.' The friar shook his head at Gisburne's folly. 'Fancy putting so few men on patrol. I suspect the men I saw were picked for brawn rather than brains. Honestly, they were making so much noise as they walked the forest path, that the Devil himself could have heard them.' Tuck flopped onto the floor to rest his feet. 'There's an atmosphere of fear there though, Robin. It's as if Papplewick is just waiting for the next disaster.'

'I know we said we wouldn't,' Much hopped from foot to foot, 'but we have to go there. Now!'

Robin indicated his agreement by issuing instructions. 'Douse the fire John. Tuck gather some food for each of us. Nasir, will you go ahead? Find a place to lookout across the whole village. Take some food and water, we may be waiting some time.'

The outlaws moved fast, but Much found himself in the middle of a hive of activity, not knowing which way to go first. He could see himself doing what he normally did when they got ready to go to someone's aid, but he wasn't actually doing it. He felt frozen. All he could think about was the possibility of it going wrong.

What if we can't save Kate's father?

'Come on, Much!' A gentle clout knocked him on the back of his head as Little John passed him some more slingshot. 'I thought you wanted us to hurry.'

As Much came to his senses, Nasir disappeared into the forest and Robin addressed the others. 'Marion, Much and I will take the far path that leads into Papplewick via the main road. We'll wait in the trees for Guy's party to arrive. When it does, we'll follow them in. John, Will, you go with Tuck. He'll show you how he got into the village.'

'And if you're wrong and Gisburne don't show?' Scarlet sheathed his sword with one hand and grabbed his knife with the other.

'Then we'll find another way,' Robin gave a determined grimace. 'When you get into the village, it's vital the people there aren't seen to be helping us. This is what I want you to do...'

***

'Kate will be alright. She sounds like a strong girl.'

'Thank you, Marion.' Much scrutinized every change in the shadows as they progressed through Sherwood. He winced as he remembered boasting to Kate about how good they were at moving silently, at listening, at avoiding trouble. Kate had copied him, learnt from him, but trouble had found her and her village anyway.

We will save your father, Kate. We will.

Stopping abruptly, Robin beckoned for the others to step into the undergrowth just in time to observe the two men Tuck and Much had seen earlier that day, blunder into view. Obviously bored of walking in circles, their grumbles about the pointlessness of the mission Gisburne had sent them on would have been enough to earn them a night or two in the dungeons, if their master had caught wind of their complaints.

Once the guards had passed by, Robin edged forward. 'There's a clump of trees near where the road forks towards the track for Papplewick. We'll wait for Gisburne there.'

Much didn't bother asking Robin how long he thought they'd be waiting. Instead he offered up a private prayer for a successful rescue to take place sooner rather than later.

Kate needs her father, Herne. Please, can you help us?

Whether Herne had noted his plea, or if Gisburne had decided to act entirely without any intervention from the forest god, the outlaws heard the rumble of cart wheels less than an hour later. Much gave his bird call in the hope Nasir would hear it as Robin raised his arm, ready to give the signal for them to strike. The air felt tight as the sound of hooves and cartwheels grew louder. They could each feel the thump of the approaching horses against the sun dried earth resound in their chests.

A single horse pulled the cart, while six soldiers rode as protection, three on either side. Gisburne was at the back, his eyes fixed on the wagon door, as if expecting it to be flung open and the prisoner attempt an escape at any moment. Two more soldiers flanked their master as they trotted briskly towards Papplewick.

On Robin's sign the three outlaws wove between the trees, keeping pace with the wagon. It wasn't until the soldiers entered the village itself that they jogged to a halt.

'We need to get closer.' Tension rippled through Much as he stared at the village. It appeared to be deserted.

'Not long now.' Marion pulled back her bow; her arm steady, ready to fire as soon as Robin gave the word.

***

The audience of frightened villagers Gisburne had expected to rush from their homes on his arrival hadn't arrived.

Circling his horse impatiently, frustrated that there was no one to browbeat, he yelled across the eerily quiet settlement. 'Get out here, you lazy swine! Why can't I see you working? This village is in enough trouble already, do you really want me to raize Papplewick to the ground?'

Despite the deputy's threat, nothing happened. Nothing moved but the birds in the sky, and even they were keeping a safe distance.

Trying not to worry about Kate, trusting Tuck, Little John and the others to have carried out Robin's plan, Much nocked an arrow to his bow. Wanting nothing more than to shoot Gisburne in revenge for frightening Kate, he tried to remember how to breathe.

CHAPTER 12

Kate sat very still. The door of the barn had been left slightly ajar, and she could see horse's hooves stamping and the parked wheels of a cart. *Father?*

The other villagers didn't seem to care what was happening outside. They were staring at the two men stood inside the barn doors; their faces grim, their tunics stuffed with an assortment of weapons, loaded bows in their hands.

Much taught me to watch and wait and listen.

Kate tried not to fidget as she looked at her neighbours. They'd done what she'd told them, but she wished she'd had time to explain the plan properly. As it was, she'd only been able to plead with them that they were doing this for her father and the safety of the village and that it would be alright. But none of them had been sure and Kate didn't blame them. For now they sat with her on the floor of the barn, their eyes wide with terror, looking every bit like the hostages Robin wanted them to appear to be, while two notorious outlaws blocked the only way out.

I wish Much had taught me to fight as well as listen.

The atmosphere in the barn was thick with fear as Sir Guy of Gisburne's voice ricocheted around Papplewick for a second time. 'I said come out here you miserable scum!'

A low rumbling of concern tripped around the villagers, but no one spoke as Will Scarlet and Little John each stretched out a leg, ready to kick the barn door open when the time came.

Hoping her neighbours would stay strong and that he memory of Friar Tuck's kindness in bringing them food when they were hungry, would give them the courage to trust the outlaws and remain where they were, Kate felt the muscles in her shoulders curl into knots. She watched Will Scarlett and Little John. They might have been there to help, but that didn't stop them appearing every bit as frightening as the soldiers tormenting the village.

They are Much's friends. They are Robin Hood's men. They are here to help us.
Kate repeated the words over and over in her head like a mantra.
I wish you were here with us, Much.

***

Gisburne had had enough.

'You two,' he signalled to the soldiers flanking the front of the cart, 'search the village.'

From the shelter of the trees, Robin watched the Sherriff's lackey.

Predictable as ever, Guy.

He knew Scarlet and John would have heard the lofty order. It was time to act.

'Now!' Robin let an arrow fly. It was chased across the sky by two more from Much and Marion. Each shaft hit their targets with a juddering thwack, sending the guards either side of Gisburne to the ground and their horses skittering into the forest, while the third arrow greeted a soldier on the nearside of the wagon square in the back.

Gisburne and the remaining soldiers struggled to control their frightened horses as the man driving the wagon leapt from his seat and disappeared into Sherwood. The other guards froze, their eyes darting into the trees, trying to work out where the outlaws were hiding.

'Wolfsheads!'

Robin marched confidently into the village with Much and Marion at his side. 'You called, Gisburne?'

'These villagers stand accused of treason for colluding with outlaws. With you!'

'What villagers?'

'What have you done with them? Where are they?'

As Gisburne blustered, Nasir dropped from a nearby tree, two swords at the ready, while Friar Tuck trotted out of a nearby hut, his quarter staff playing between his hands.

'You are, as usual, mistaken, Guy.' Robin plucked a new arrow from his quiver and placed it on his bow. 'These villagers have caused us nothing but trouble. They are, in fact our prisoners, and will be until I say otherwise.'

Letting the arrow fly, it hit the sturdy wood barn doors, which immediately flew open in response. Will Scarlet and Little John stormed out, their weapons drawn. Behind them, in three neat rows, sat the villagers of Papplewick, their hands behind their backs, their mouths closed, their expressions a mixture of defiance and fear.

'Your prisoners?' Gisburne's eyes narrowed suspiciously. 'Since when did the so-called people's hero start taking innocent people prisoner?'

'Oh, so you admit they're innocent do you? Thank you, Guy.' Robin's voice rose as he called across to Will and John, 'it seems we were mistaken. Gisburne says these people have done nothing wrong, so we'd better let them go.' Then with his tone as smooth as honey, Robin twisted his attention back to the Sheriff's deputy. 'We clearly made a mistake. But while we're here Guy, why don't you tell me why you have one of these *innocent* villagers locked in that cart?'

'I never said any of them were innocent!'

'Don't shout at me, Guy.' Robin kept talking as Much swung round so the arrow on his bow was pointing straight at Gisburne's heart. 'Why is it that you like to play Sheriff so much while your master's away? I'm sure De Rainault will be thrilled when he gets back to Nottingham. The gossip of your latest failure is sure to have reached his ears by the time he gets home.'

'And he'll hear how you took an entire village hostage!' Gisburne signalled to his men, who ran at the outlaws.

***

From the floor of the barn, Kate watched in horror as soldiers surrounded the prison wagon. She clamped her mouth shut, biting her lips together so that she didn't let Much down by crying out and distracting the outlaws. Cramped up next to her neighbours on the floor, it was so hard not to get to her feet and hurl stones or anything she could grab from the side of the barn, at the assailants. Yet, in the same breath, she daren't move. Will Scarlet and Little John had cautioned them all to stay where they were. Twice they'd repeated that, if they sat still and didn't join in the fight, they couldn't be accused of any wrongdoing. It was important for the village's future safety to be seen not to be helping the outlaws, even appearing to be their prisoners.

Kate tried not to seek Much out as the fight continued, but she couldn't help it.

Stay safe, Much, stay safe…

Her eyes wide with fear, Kate watched helplessly as a soldier ran forward and tried to grab Marion, only to almost cheer as Much came to his friend's aid. At some point in the fight he'd dropped his bow, and now his sling was taking aim and a face full of jagged grit had spattered across the retreating soldier.

Will Scarlet and Little John were battling furiously with swords and quarter staff. The noise was deafening as the stamp of boots and hooves made the rickety barn quiver right to its rafters. Horses whinnied and metal and wood clashed. Kate closed her eyes, wondering how her father was coping. Trapped, listening to the chaos outside, but not knowing what was happening, and worse, not being able to do anything about it.

Seconds later, the barn floor shuddered beneath her and the woman next to her screamed. Kate's eyes flew back open as a guard grabbed her by the shoulder.

Dragged from the barn towards the battle outside Kate wanted to yell, to shout and kick, but there was a knife at her throat. The blade caressed her skin and a stone cold fear crept up her spine, paralysing her muscles.

Much saw Kate first. His yell of 'No!' ricocheted across the village.

Gisburne laughed as Robin also noticed the young woman at the end of a soldier's knife. 'Time to drop your weapons wolfsheads.'

The jarring clatter of metal and wood as bows, staves, slings and swords hit the ground, was instant. Marion placed a hand on Much's shoulder, her unspoken warning forcing him to fight his instinct to hurtle towards Kate.

Robin kept his eyes on Gisburne. His tone was icily calm. 'When you leave here and ride on to Newark, I want you to deliver a message to the Sheriff. It's time he stopped accusing every village in the forest of theft, when we all know *he* is the biggest thief around here.'

Gisburne scoffed. 'Are you blind, wolfshead? There's a girl with her throat about to be cut over there. All I have to do is give the order.'

'I think *you* are the blind one, Guy! Look around you. How many men do you have left standing?'

The split second of confusion Robin's comment caused as the remaining guards glanced warily about the village, taking in the number of their fallen comrades, was all that was needed.

Two previously hidden knives flew from Nasir's hands. One drove deep into the leg of the soldier nearest Gisburne, while the other buried itself into the chest of Kate's warder.

Recoiling from the sickening strike of the knife, her legs trembling, Kate resisted the urge to sag to the floor as her neck was freed from the caress of metal. Instead she kicked the stricken soldier in the centre of his right knee and ran towards Much.

She was three paces away from him, when she spotted the frantic warning on Will's face and realised her mistake. Everyone had warned her, when they'd arrived in Papplewick, about the danger of letting it be known that they knew any of the outlaw's personally - a danger that would never go away if Gisburne noticed an association between them.

Hoping she hadn't given herself away, Kate changed direction. Darting back into the barn, she flopped down next to her friends, her whole body shaking. Even then, she only allowed herself to cry when she heard Robin ask Nasir to open the wagon.

As a bedraggled William was helped from the cart, blinking in the sunshine after so many hours in the dark, Gisburne shouted at his men. 'To Newark!'

Marion moved quickly, her bow pulled and her arrow on target as Robin stepped in front of Gisburne. Grabbing his horses' bridle, Robin snarled, 'I mentioned a message.'

'If you think I'm going to be your messenger boy…'

'You will be what I tell you to be!'

'Don't play the Earl's son with me outlaw!'

'And don't play the fool with me, Guy!' Robin shouted back. 'Tell the Sheriff that the people of Papplewick, after you murdered David and his family, cut all ties with us. I will not allow these people to be continually punished for something they no longer do. Something, that only your master's greed forced them into doing in the first place.'

'I told you! We have proof they have taken money from you to pay their taxes! And why would you expect me to believe what you say when here you are! You're helping them now!'

'We are here because we bumped into a friend of yours, Harold his name was.' Robin noticed a nudging amongst the remaining guards as a cloud passed over Gisburne's face. 'He was keen to tell me about how you've started using your own men as bait. An interesting idea.'

The murmuring amongst the guards increased.

'Silence! He's trying to confuse you.' Gisburne glared at his men. 'That doesn't explain why you're here, now.'

'True.' Darting forward, Robin grabbed hold of Gisburne's cloak and pulled him to the ground, holding him up by his collar. 'He's a talkative man, Harold, when he's had a drink. He mentioned you'd taken a prisoner, one who'd done nothing wrong, and that you planned to use him to scare the villagers away from us.'

Taking Gisburne's sword, Robin called to Scarlet to help him. Moments later, thrashing his limbs and protesting at the top of his voice, the Sheriff's deputy was stripped of all but his undergarments and thrown across his saddle.

'Bind his hands, Will. Maybe he'll learn some humility on the way to Newark.'

'How about these two, Robin?' John asked, as he and Tuck came forward, holding the only two soldiers that were neither dead, injured, or had had the good sense to run away. 'Shall we chuck 'em in the ditch?'

'Why not?' Keeping his eyes fixed upon Gisburne, Robin said, 'Tell me the message you are going to deliver to De Rainault.'

Guy's eyes blazed hatred as he spat, 'The Sheriff is to leave Papplewick alone.'

Scarlet grinned. 'I always knew he 'ad to be cleverer than he looked.'

OCTOBER

CHAPTER 13

Much listened to the wind swaggering through the forest, testing and stretching its power as Sherwood waved goodbye to the final traces of summer and fully embraced autumn.

He'd been in the meeting place for only a few minutes when Kate appeared through the trees. He smiled. He hadn't heard her approach. She'd learnt a lot about survival since they'd met seven months ago.

'Much! I didn't think you'd be here.'

'Why not?

'Well, after all the fighting. Oh, I still can't believe it worked! Thank you. Thank you!' Kate clapped with pleasure. 'And to the others of course. You were all so wonderful.'

Much, who'd been bursting with pride for Kate since they'd watched Gisburne trail off to Newark in disgrace, found her enthusiasm contagious. 'You were fantastic. Robin was impressed. I's sure you could some stay with us… if you wanted to. The way you kicked that soldier after he'd drag you out of the barn! You really was amazing.'

'I did, didn't I. I can't quite believe it.'

More serious, as he remembered the reason they'd had to fight the soldiers in the first place, he asked, 'how is your father, now?'

Shuffling closer to Much, Kate gave a half smile. 'Better. But how did Robin know the Sheriff had him in Nottingham Castle?'

'Goodwill.'

'Sorry?'

'Like this.' Much patted the sack Kate had bought with her and then jangled the money bag at his belt, 'The villagers we help might exchange a few vegetables or something for the money they need to pay their taxes, but what we mostly gets in return is information. That's how we find stuff out. That's how Nasir heard about your father being transferred from Nottingham castle to Newark. He met some villagers travelling through Sherwood and they told him.'

The instant of levity passed as Kate explained, 'Gisburne told Father that the Sheriff suspected him of stealing cos we always had the tax money ready on time.' She paused as she remembered how shaken her father was by his experience in Nottingham's dungeon. 'They were going to send him to fight in a war as punishment... but it was you who stole...'

'Which is why we were so determined to rescue your father. Robin was sure Gisburne wouldn't be able to resist driving the prison wagon through Papplewick so he could gloat at your family and friends.'

'I'm glad he did. If not... I don't like to think about it. My father is no fighter. He'd have been killed for sure. What would I have done then?'

Much didn't even pause. He knew exactly what he'd have wanted to happen. 'You'd come and live with me in the forest.' Suddenly less certain, he added, 'but only if you'd wanted to.'

'Thank you, Much.' Kate's eyes shone as, acting on an impulse, she leant in and planted a light kiss on his cheek so quickly, that Much hadn't seen it coming.

As the outlaw's complexion blossomed like a newly grown apple, Kate grinned shyly, 'you okay, Much?'

'Uh-huh... Not been kissed by a girl before... Umm...yeah, so did you see the way Little John and Tuck knocked the Sheriff's men that were left at the end into the village ditch? I bet they stank for ages.'

Giggling, Kate added, 'and the way Robin threatened Gisburne! Saying he wasn't to take any more innocent villagers when he knows exactly who the thief is - the Sheriff for demanding too much of us in the first place. I almost cheered! You was great too, Much... I saw you sling shot that soldier as he tried to grab Marion! We're all going to be safe forever and ever now cos of you.'

Shuffling awkwardly, Much mumbled, 'yeah, well, I hope so. Stay careful though won't you, Kate. Don't forget what I've taught you. Gisburne don't like being laughed at, and we laughed at him a lot when Robin and Will threw him across his horse in just his next to nethers!'

The laughter died on Kate's lips as she asked, 'you think he'll come back?'

'Gisburne always comes back. But don't worry; I'll take care of you. Are you cold? You look cold.'

'A bit.'

'Um,' Much swallowed, 'I could warm you up... if you wanted. A hug, I mean... if you want me to.'

Moving with speed, before he could change his mind, Kate pressed her slight frame against Much's side. 'Of course I want you to.'

Slipping his arm around Kate's shoulder, noting how perfectly she fitted into the space, Much whispered, 'Oh, well… that's nice then.' They lapsed into silence, listening to the breeze as it tickled the leaves above them.

NOVEMBER

CHAPTER 14

'When did William say he heard the guard talking about the next movement of tax money towards London?' Little John let the few remaining coins from the previous raid trickle through his fingers.

'Not until after the worst of the winter.'

'But that's weeks away.'

Tuck dropped five marks into a money pouch and passed it to Much. 'For Kate tomorrow.'

Thanking the friar, hoping his eagerness to see Kate didn't show on his face, Much asked John, 'how come William knew that?'

'The guards who took him from Nottingham dungeon and threw him into the prison wagon talked as if he wasn't there.'

'They probably assumed he'd be dead by the following day. No point in keeping secrets from a condemned man.' Robin threw some wood onto the fire. 'William's account ties in with what Harold said about their being a late winter tax collection to send to the king.'

Much's body tensed. He didn't like to think about how close they'd come to losing Kate her father just because they had been trying to help. He was about to say so, when he noticed the concern on Robin's face. 'Are you alright, Robin?'

'It's been too easy.'

'What do you mean?' Scarlet came nearer to the fire.

Seeing he was unsure about sharing his concerns when he didn't really understand them himself, Marion said, 'come on, Robin. Talk to us. It's obvious something's bothering you. You've been preoccupied ever since we left Papplewick almost three weeks ago.'

Throwing a second log onto the crackling blaze, Robin grimaced, 'it could just be me, just a feeling, but...'

'But what?' Marion coaxed. 'Your feelings haven't let us down before.'

'As I said, it's all been a bit too easy lately.'

'Easy?' Will was astounded. 'Oh, sure. Fighting Gisburne's men, risking our lives every day for strangers, not knowing what hell lies around the corner. Dead easy that is.'

'Straight forward rather than easy, then.' Used to Scarlet's sarcasm, Robin went on, 'then there was what Harold said, plus, did you notice the look on the guards faces in Papplewick when I said we'd seen Harold? Not to mention on Gisburne's expression?'

'Gisburne did look a bit cross when you asked 'im about 'arold. Crosser than usual I mean.' Much pulled a face as he considered the Sheriff's deputy, 'I reckon the other guards knew 'arold had run away from a life of service with the Sheriff.'

Robin nodded. 'That sort of information could be dangerous. Why do you think I sent Guy on his way without them? I hope they had the sense to run away too.'

Silence descended on the group as they considered what Robin had said. At the time it had felt like a normal fight. Gisburne had been making a villager's life hell and so they'd done something about it. But now…The fire crackled and popped as the weather blustered its way through the trees, as if it was waiting alongside the outlaws to hear what Robin had to say.

'When we've stopped the tax wagon, there hasn't been as much money as usual.'

'Perhaps the Sheriff has been ordered not to collect so much from the people.' Much suggested, earning himself a look of disbelief from Will and a kind, but nonetheless annoying, shake of the head from Robin. 'Unlikely, although I wish that were true.'

'Well, what then!?' Much snapped. 'Are you saying we shouldn't have helped Kate and her father?'

'Of course not!' Robin ruffled a hand through his hair in exasperation, 'but the fact remains that the last twice we've stopped the tax wagon, it has only been guarded by a few men, and they have retreated fast. One look at us and they've all but fled. Usually Gisburne makes an effort to save the Sheriff's money, so why didn't he order his men to put up a fight?'

'Cos there was less money to bovver about.' Will took a swig from his ale.

'Maybe.' Robin shrugged. 'Then there's what Herne said. It was months ago but however I work it, I can't see how it makes sense. Yet, I'm still convinced it's to do with Papplewick and the tax money.

'What *did* Herne say?' Tuck asked as he passed some bowls of stew around the fire.

'"Nothing easily won is worth the battle. Lay down the bow to find the marks."'

'My old mum used to stay stuff like that all the time,' Will grunted. 'Means nothing.'

Smiling at the image of Will's mother spinning her son some home truths, Robin said, 'I can't shift the feeling it's a trap, but it can't be, because no one's tried to trap us.'

'Yet,' pressed Will.

Robin continued. 'And if it *is* a trap, it has to be one we aren't supposed to fight our way out of. Herne said; lay down our bow to find the mark.'

''Arold!' Much sat bolt upright from where he'd been sat fiddling with his knife, half listening, half wondering if Kate would kiss him again. 'That's what he said, remember Robin? 'Arold said they was trap meat.'

'I know, but...'

Much cut across Robin. 'And you was just saying about seeing Gisburne's face when you mentioned 'Arold and using men as bait. What if Guy wasn't worried about you knowing that one of his men had runaway and him losing face? What if he's worried that 'Arold told you about the tax money...which he did a bit, didn't he...although not a lot of it made sense.' Talking faster and faster, Much felt sure he was onto something. 'Maybe Gisburne is thinking that 'Arold knew something more than he did.'

John leant forward, 'but why would the Sheriff be putting his own men in a trap?'

'Not in a trap, John,' Robin felt a trickle if understanding at last, 'but *baiting* a trap. Much is right. I think our runaway did know more. You don't give up shelter and wages just as winter gets a grip unless you're afraid of what might happen if you don't. What if Harold was scared, not about knowing what the Sheriff was up to, but of the Sheriff finding out he knew about it?'

'So he was running from the wrath of the Sheriff discovering he'd been where he wasn't supposed to be and overhearing something he shouldn't have heard, rather than of what he was being forced to do.' Marion nodded.

'Yes, although I don't think he liked that much either.' Robin scooped up a spoonful of stew and emptied it again, watching as the meat landed with a helpless splash into the bowl. 'What if it isn't *us* the Sheriff is trying to trap, but the people we help?'

Much was paying full attention now. 'Papplewick?'

'Yes.' A trickle of certainty tripped down Robin's spine as he put down his food and picked up one of the bags of tax money meant for the villagers. 'Gisburne said he had proof that William of Papplewick was taking money from us, but we know he hasn't seen us at the village with any money. And you *have* been careful haven't you, Much?'

'Very careful. And I's taught Kate to be careful, too.'

'So the only question now is,' Robin poured the coins into his hand, tightly cupping the discs of metal, 'what proof is Gisburne talking about?'

***

The early morning sky fired a persistent drizzle onto Much's hood as he waited for Kate. The days and hours until they'd been due to meet again had passed cripplingly slowly. He wasn't sure how he'd managed not to go to Papplewick to find her, or to at least hide in the trees and see if he could catch a glimpse of Kate going about her daily life. Knowing his desire to reassure himself that she was safe was as risky as it was good intentioned, Much had stuck it out; counting off the days. Perhaps it was good that the outlaws' had been so busy lately.

The onset of winter always bought increased need from the poorest folk of Sherwood and Nottingham. The foresters in particular, revelled in taking out the discomforts caused by the encroaching daily frosts on the people, handing out swifter and harsher penalties for minor infractions of the law with each fresh decrease in temperature.

Much wished Robin would cheer up. He'd done nothing but pace up and down since yesterday's camp fire discussion, murmuring about having to learn about the proof Gisburne claimed he had and what the consequences might be for all the villages if they didn't.

He pulled his hood further over his face, watching the drips fall from its rim.

Kate will come today. She will. Gisburne's busy in Newark and the weather has been too awful for troublemakers. Kate will *come today.*

A noise from the tree above made Much jump and he drew his knife.

A twig fell to the ground in front of him. He tutted in relief and he put his blade away. 'Thanks a lot tree. You scared me to death.'

Another stick fell, accompanied by the sound of a stiffed chuckle, which made Much look up into the rain. 'What?'

'Boo!' Swinging from the tree to the ground, Kate threw her sack at Much's feet.

Laughing out loud, Much beamed, 'you're getting too good at that! How long have you been up there?'

'Ages!' She pointed to the sack, 'there's cabbages in the sack.'

'Oh dear.' Much wrinkled his nose.

'Oh dear?'

Much winked, 'Cabbages make Tuck go a bit smelly.'

Laughing harder, Kate pulled a sympathetic face, 'maybe I will forget to give them to you.' Tilting her head to one side, she asked, 'why didn't you think I'd come?'

Much found he couldn't look at Kate as he muttered, 'You might have decided you didn't like being hugged.'

'Well, I did like it. Can I have another one?'

DECEMBER

CHAPTER 15

Snow deadened the natural sounds of the forest as Much huddled under the blankets he'd brought with him in case Kate was chilly. Soon he heard someone traipsing nearer, but it wasn't the light footfall he'd been expecting.

As William of Papplewick strode into the clearing, Much pushed back the hide covers and clambered to his feet. 'Sir?'

'Much, I'm glad I found you. Kate gave me the directions, but without her I wasn't sure I'd reach you through the snow.'

'Where's Kate? Is she safe?' A sense of dread crept over Much as he took in William's sallow face.

'She has a fever. I… I'm not sure…' His voice cracked. 'A week ago, Papplewick was hit with a terrible malady and now Kate… She's all I have.'

Much knew William would be thinking of his recently deceased wife, Martha, and what life would be like if he lost his beloved child as well. He passed his companion a blanket to wrap around his shoulders. 'Come on. We're going to fetch Marion, and then we're going to Papplewick.'

'What can Marion do?'

'Marion is going to save Kate. Because if not… if not…' Much marched out of the clearing with William close at his heels. 'Marion *is* going to save my Kate. She'll know what to do… and Tuck too. They'll know. They always know…Come on!'

They'd only reached the edge of the meeting place when common sense nudged through Much's sense of panic. 'No, you should go back to Kate. She needs you, and anyway, if you're spotted with me that'll bring you more trouble. I'll arrange help.'

William shook Much's hand hard. 'Thank you, my friend.'

***

'But I ought to go too!'

'And put Kate in more danger, not to mention the people of Papplewick? You know what happened last time they were suspected of helping us!' Robin hated having to argue with Much when he knew how worried he was about his friend. Lowering his voice, he said, 'I do understand, I really do,' Robin's eyes fell on Marion as she and Tuck busied themselves once again with collecting supplies for the villagers, 'but it's risky enough sending two of us.'

'But...'

'If the soldiers see you with Kate then they'll know. They'll see she's important to you just by the way you look at each other. And you know what happens then, Much.'

Flushing pink, Much dropped the bag of blankets he'd collected to take to Papplewick. He wished that Robin wasn't right almost as much as he wished Kate wasn't sick in the first place. Turning to Marion, he opened his mouth to speak, to ask her to pass a message to Kate, but no words would come.

Guessing what he was going to say, Marion gave Much a trusting smile. 'We'll do everything we can, I promise.'

'She must be okay, she must. For William's sake.' He didn't add for his own. Friar Tuck laid a hand on Much's shoulder. 'That's not our decision to make, but we'll try our best and tell her you're thinking of her.'

Inclining his head, determined not to let his friends know just how worried he was, Much tried to remember what Kate had said about getting in and out the village.

'I asked Kate about the best chance of getting into Papplewick unnoticed last time I saw her. She said that, at the back of the village, there's a narrow path in.' He glanced briefly at Tuck, hoping that his friend's barrel shaped figure would fit along it, and felt he ought to stress the point. 'I mean, it's ever such a thin track according to Kate. It'll take you from the forest to behind the village barn. If you follow the east fork once you get to the meeting place, then weave through the trees, following the slope of the land, you should find it.'

Tuck patted his belly affectionately. 'Perhaps I'll send Marion down the very thin path first, in case I get wedged.'

***

Much watched until his friends blended into the embrace of the forest.

He'd never felt so useless in his life. There were loads of jobs to do around the camp, but although he desperately wanted to be busy to fill the time until Marion and Tuck returned, he couldn't settle.

Watching Much sitting listlessly by the fire, Robin beckoned to Little John. 'He needs distracting.'

'Aye, he does.'

'Take him fishing, John. Talk to him. He might open up to you.'

'Take him fishing?' Leaning on his staff, John regarded Robin as if he'd received a blow to the head. 'It's been snowing lad! And it is flippin' freezing. Any fish will be so deep in the river we'll have no chance of catching anything. Besides,' he sighed, 'what would I say to him?'

'John, you know Much better than any of us. You don't have to say anything, just be there.'

***

The air above the water hung heavy with a frost, which tasted sharp at the back of the outlaws throats. But for the occasional drip of melting ice, the small lake was eerily still beneath the shelter of Sherwood's snow-laden trees.

Little John nodded approvingly. 'That's it, lower the rod a fraction more… yes lad. Now, here you go,' he passed Much a heavy lump of fallen wood. 'Trap the rod beneath this. That'll keep it in place so the line can do its magic by itself while we get warm by the fire.'

Sitting close to the blaze John had constructed from dry kindling he'd carried from the camp, Much watched as his friend double checked the line. 'We won't catch anything will we?'

'Probably not. Good practise for you though. Fishing's never been your strong point.'

Much gave a rueful grin as John joined him. 'That's true. Remember when I fell into the Trent trying to fish with Tuck last year?'

John barked with laughter. 'So you did. Your face! Will and I never could decide if you were more shocked at the cold water or just plain cross.' Laying down his quarter staff, Little John regarded his friend. He couldn't help wishing Robin had found something else for Much to do.

'John?'

'Yes, lad.'

'Do you remember when we was shepherds?'

Lifting his palms nearer to the flickering orange heat, John's concern increased. Much rarely mentioned their time in Hathersage. ''Course I do.'

'Did you, umm…' Much paused, unsure whether to continue.

'Go on lad, what is it?'

'Well, Meg wasn't there was she, and I know you two is close friends.'

John cleared his throat, buying himself thinking time. 'Yeah, we're close friends.'

'We didn't know did we, that we'd be coming back to Sherwood, I mean?' Much pulled his hood further over his head so John couldn't see the growing blush on his face. 'We believed we'd be there forever with them sheep. Always looking over our shoulders, always waiting for someone to find us and throw us in chains.'

'That we did.' John stared into the fire as the spectre of Robin of Loxley's death, the reason for their temporary exile, fell across them, cooling the air the fire had been battling so hard to defrost.

'But, Meg...did you miss her while we were there?'

The sound that escaped John's lips was ragged and for a second Much was afraid he'd made his friend angry, but he needn't have worried. Reaching out a hand, John gave Much a reassuring shove. 'Marion and Tuck will do all they can for Kate, you know that don't you.'

'Yeah, yeah I know.' Trailing a finger across the top of his boots, Much knocked off the snow that clung to the leather as he added, 'and then...then you was gonna leave us and go off with Meg. Before King John got us and we nearly got our 'eads chopped off. You remember that don't you John; after we helped with them pigs?'

Much lifted his simple, eager and anxious face to John, but he wasn't sure his companion had heard anything he'd said. Wishing he hadn't mentioned Meg, but knowing he couldn't undo what was done, Much studied the snow melting around the fire. 'One was called Rutterkin. Good name for a pig, that.'

When he finally spoke, Little John's voice was so quiet, that at first Much thought he was talking to himself. 'I told myself I'd go back for Meg eventually, while we were in Hathersage. See if she'd leave Wickham and come to live with us. But as time passed I made myself believe she'd be safer where she was, in Wickham with Edward and the others, rather than living with the likes of us.'

Then the gentlest man he'd ever known looked Much straight in the eyes, silently pleading with him to understand. 'That's why we didn't leave together after King John almost..., you know... How could I ask Meg to face a fate like that?'

'You missed her though, when we was being shepherds?'

'Much, Meg lives in Wickham. It's less than an hour's walk away but I miss her every day.' John exhaled noisily, guttering the flames. 'I can't go and see her whenever I feel like it. I can't be with her because I'm an outlaw. She might as well live in Scotland!'

Knowing John was speaking the truth, and that no amount of wishing he wasn't would change anything, Much mumbled, 'I shouldn't see Kate should I? When she's better, I should leave her in peace. You could take the goodwill to her instead.'

John threw an extra twig on the fire. 'If only letting go was that easy.' He gave Much a sad smile. 'See her when you can. When it's safe. Take no risks - ever. Take comfort in knowing she's out there. That someone in the forest is thinking of you as you, rather than you as one of Robin Hood's men. I can't wish you more than that Much, but I would if I could.'

'I didn't mean this to happen. I didn't even want to go and meet Kate the first time and now I...'

'I know lad. I know.'

As they lapsed into a melancholy hush, Much was knocked from his contemplation by the tremble of the fishing line. 'John, the rod! It moved.'

'Can't have.' The line quivered again and John leapt up. 'Come on, lad, pull it out the water. Careful now.'

Not a minute later and Much was proudly showing off a perch that wriggled helplessly on the end of the line. John clapped him on the back. 'Will you look at that? In the middle of winter, too. Maybe it's a day for miracles.'

Much smiled at his friend. 'Let's hope so.'

JANUARY

CHAPTER 16

Kate burst into the clearing. Despite her thick cloak and the extra layers of clothes she wore as protection against the harsh New Year weather, Much could tell she'd lost weight. Her face was pinched and her usual ruddy glow was missing.

'Much! I'm so glad to see you.' Her smile extinguished all signs of her recent suffering.

'Are you better? You were so ill, I was worried.' Wrapped up in as many cloaks as she was, Much passed another to Kate to pull around her shoulders. Much shifted along the freezing trunk, showing her how he'd padded the wood in blankets.

'Marion and Tuck saved me. I'm sure they did. And the others what had the fever.'

His tone flat, Much muttered, 'yeah. Good.'

'What's wrong?' Kate snuggled into his side.

'Nothing.'

'Much?' Kate wasn't convinced.

'I'd have liked to be the one to save you, that's all.' He grumbled into his cloak, his breath sending puffs of frozen breath into the winter air. 'I pretend I'm important, but I'm not. Not really. I do all the little jobs. The stuff that doesn't matter. They don't need me, I'm just there. Anyone could do what I do.'

Threading a hand into Much's cloak pocket so she could hold his hand, Kate's eyes shone with happiness. 'But you *did* save me.'

Much squeezed her soft palm. 'I did?'

'Of course you did. If you hadn't sent Marion and Friar Tuck to the village with their 'erbs and stuff I could have died.'

'I wanted to visit, too, but Robin said no. Said it would bring trouble if one of Gisburne's men spotted me visiting you.'

'Robin was sensible and I wouldn't have wanted to risk you catching the fever, so I's glad you stayed safe. Can I cuddle up against you now to make up for it?'

''Course.'

'It's so *cold*.' Kate snuggled even closer, throwing part of her extra cloak over their knees. 'That's better. Anyway, soldiers have been keeping an eye on us. I think the Sheriff knows your helping the village again and is trying to catch you and your friends in the act.'

Much sighed again. 'Robin was right to stop me then. He's usually right, but I still would have liked to help you more.'

'When my mother was alive she used to say that lots of little helpful things make the big things and the best things. I think she was right.'

'She sounds nice.'

'She was. I miss her. What about you? Do you have parents?'

Much looked up at the sky. The white mists that coated the air were beginning to thin and, as he watched, a chink in the clouds gave way to a single patch of cornflower blue. Friar Tuck would have said it was a sign of hope for the better weather to come. Maybe it was a sign, a sign he should tell Kate about his family; a story he never told anyone. A memory that even the outlaws left alone.

'That is a very long story.'

Noting the sad lilt that had crept into Much's voice, Kate linked her fingers through his and kissed his numb cheek. 'Tell me.'

His voice was barely audible when the words came. It felt strange to be saying them aloud rather than just thinking them. 'My parents was millers. It was just them and me, and my adopted brother, Robin.'

'Robin? Like Robin Hood?'

Much exhaled. 'Exactly like Robin Hood. His name was Robin of Loxley. He came to live with us at the mill after the Sheriff had killed his father, Ailric. Robin was older than me, and cleverer, but we was still like brothers.' He paused as Kate held his hand tighter.

'One day he saved me from Gisburne after I'd shot a deer. We ended up in the Sheriff's dungeon in the castle. Same one your father was in. Will Scarlet was already in there and so was… we made other friends in there too…'

Much closed his eyes as faces from his past filled him up. He felt he could reach out and touch them. He could see Dickon laughing and Tom's trusting smile. Much kept talking, scared to stop in case emotion got the better of him, assured that Kate wouldn't judge him for the mistakes he'd made. He told her how, if he hadn't shot one of the King's deer in the first place they might never have been made outlaws, and how… when the end had come, it had been Marion and him that Robin of Loxley had died for.

'I'll never forget his last words to me, Kate. I can hear them as if he were speaking them now. He said, "I'm putting all my trust in you, Much. You won't fail me will you?"'

Much swallowed against the emotion rising in his chest. 'Even then, when Robin said that, I couldn't believe he was going to let the Sheriff's men shoot him. But if he hadn't, Marion and me…we'd be…'

Kate held Much close as he talked. She didn't know what to say as he stared into the middle distance, not seeing anything beyond the boy he had once been.

'Then, like a miracle, Robert of Huntingdon came. He found us and bought us back together, and well, here we are.'

Reaching out, Kate stroked Much's face, removing the single tear that had escaped, despite his efforts to stay strong. 'He'd be proud of you, your Robin of Loxley.'

'Do you really think so?' Much rested his head on her shoulder. Sharing episodes from his past had left him as exhausted as if he'd run from one side of Sherwood to the other.

'You swore you wouldn't fail him and you haven't. You're still here, still helping the people of Sherwood. Helping my people. Helping me. You've kept your promise to Robin of Loxley, Much.'

'And I always will. Always.'

FEBRUARY

CHAPTER 17

I need to be sure.

Robin looked up at Nasir in the tree above. The Saracen barely blinked as he observed the road, waiting with the patience of forever for the expected tax wagon to arrive.

Pulling a coin from his pocket, Robin Hood closed his eyes, rotating the disc carefully between his fingers. His expression was grim as he thought about Herne's words.

It wasn't to hit the mark, it was marks. Marks as in money.

'They're coming.' Nasir leapt lightly to the ground.

Robin slipped the coin away, 'this may go just like the last two tax money raids did. But if Gisburne was rattled after our encounter in Papplewick, there may be more to this wagon than a chest of tax money. Be careful.'

Concealed amongst the trees at the crossroads between Nottingham and the long road to Leicester, they waited. No one spoke until the dry still air was disturbed by the dust kicked up by horse's hooves and cartwheels.

As the convoy came into view, Marion laid a hand on Robin's arm. 'The men at the front...aren't they the two John and Tuck threw into the ditch at Papplewick?'

'I didn't see their faces' Robin glanced at John. 'Is that them?'

'Aye, that's them.'

Friar Tuck squinted in the convoy's direction, agreeing with John. 'Odd though. We don't normally recognise the soldiers as individuals. There's just too many of them.'

Much whispered. 'Maybe Gisburne is running out. That'd be good.'

Marion gave him a kind smile, 'I doubt it, Much.'

Robin however, regarded the youngest outlaw with respect. 'I think you might be right, Much.'

'You think the Sheriff is running out of men to hunt us?'

'No, but I do think he or Gisburne have decided which of their men are disposable. The ones that they can manage more easily without if they're killed on duty.'

Disgusted, Marion pulled a face. 'Just when I thought the Sheriff couldn't sink any lower.'

Keeping his gaze on the advancing wagon, Scarlet muttered, 'you think he's using the same men every time he sends out the taxes, or for mission that involves us, and not replacing the dead ones?'

There was no time for Robin to reply. Their target was now fully in sight. He frowned as he saw that the familiar guards at the front of the cart were only joined by two others. Gisburne and one further soldier rode several paces behind the group.

Will's right. Not only is the Sheriff using specific men like bait in a trap, he isn't replacing the ones who've fallen. Robin thought, too, about Harold and his plan to escape from the Sheriff by fleeing into Wales. *I hope you made it, my friend.*

'I don't want any of the guards killed.'

Will looked at Robin like he was mad. 'How can we guarantee that?'

'We can't.' Robin levelled his eyes on the distant figure of Sir Guy of Gisburne. 'But we can try our best.'

The wagon had almost passed them by when Robin gave the word to strike. Firing a volley of arrows into the rickety vehicles wooden sides before breaking cover, the outlaws had only taken a step towards their quarry when one of the guards saw Little John striding in his direction, quarter staff to hand. No doubt still embarrassed after their last encounter, he yelled to his comrades. 'It's them! Run for your lives!'

In an instant, the four men who were supposed to be protecting the tax money had fled. They had ridden away at such speed, that there was no time for Gisburne to do anything other than scream after them. Only when the lone guard accompanying him saw sense and circled his own horse back to face Nottingham, did Gisburne take note of the longbow stretched menacingly in his direction, and followed his men's example.

'You were right, Robin. That was too easy.' Will kept an eye out for movement in the trees while Tuck and Marion opened the cart.

'One box, just like last time.' Tuck pulled it close, 'but it's lighter.' He eased open the lid and showed the contents to Robin. 'Less than half full.'

'So where's the rest of it?' John poked a finger through the meagre offering.

'I'm not sure there is any rest of it.' Robin stared at the coffer. 'Let's leave the cart and get this back to camp. I'll explain there.'

***

'Where are your men Gisburne?'

De Rainault sipped at his claret suspiciously as he watched Gisburne dismount. The wine was too strong and rather bitter. After only two drafts his head was beginning to thump.

Gritting his teeth against the inevitable onslaught of anger, Gisburne patted his favourite horse's mane. 'Gone, my lord.'

'Hood killed them all?'

'They fled, my lord.'

'And you let them go?'

Gisburne rounded on the Sheriff, his temper frayed. 'How was I supposed to stop them?'

Unable to answer the question, De Rainault took another gulp of wine, before spitting it out again. 'I don't suppose it matters anyway. Now there should be enough marked coins to be able to trace every single village that is receiving its tax payments direct from Robin Hood. A brilliant plan. King John will be thrilled.'

'Thank you, my lord.'

'Why are you thanking me, Gisburne? I don't remember this being *your* idea.'

***

Robin checked every coin. Twisting and turning each one, smoothing his fingertips over each rounded edge.

It was clever; there was no doubt about that. He closed his eyes, relieved that he'd worked out what the Sheriff was planning, but that didn't extinguish his concern.

He had a horrible feeling that it was already too late. The damage was done. He wished he'd worked it out before Much had set off to find Kate.

CHAPTER 18

Panting hard as he ran, Much ducked low, wishing trees kept their leaves all year round so that he could hide in them. He kept going, avoiding the path completely.

Thankful the heavy snow of the previous month had given way to a crisp sharp frost, making it easier to hear if he was being followed, but more of a risk to be heard himself. Much shot a glance over his shoulder. There was no one in sight.

Please still be there, still be there… Herne protect Kate from harm… and me!

Much stopped moving, his heart was beating so fast it thudded in his ears. He wasn't far from the meeting place.

Have I outrun them?

Waiting, statue-like, Much peered back at the track way he'd skirted as he'd fled from the soldiers. There was still no one in sight. With a final scan through the trees, he jogged forward, stumbling through the thin trunks into the clearing.

As Much appeared, Kate flew to her feet. 'Hello! I…'

Her voice sounded unnaturally loud and he hurriedly hushed her, placing a finger on her lips.

Immediately on the alert, Kate mouthed, 'what is it?'

'Soldiers. Five of them. On foot. Think I outran them.'

Suddenly pale, Kate clutched Much's hand as they backed against the tree furthest from the clearing's entrance. 'You sure?'

Much pointed upwards. 'We must climb the tree to check. You first.'

Alarmed, Kate looked up. 'But there's no leaves to conceal us.'

'Go high.'

All hopes that Much was joking; that any second now he'd tell her he was messing about, that he was testing to discover how she reacted to see if she was good enough to join the outlaws, dissolved in the face of his earnest expression.

Placing a foot on the side of the nearest trunk, Kate let Much push her up as her feet scrabbled against the bark, and her arms stretched to grab the nearest branches. When she was about halfway up, he called quietly, 'can you take my bow?'

Hauling it up after her, Kate mouthed, 'I've got it. Come on!'

Much had just reached the tree's bare canopy when they heard footsteps and the soldiers came into view. Kate clamped her lips closed, fearful she might breathe too loud or accidentally make a noise and give them away.

Keeping his eyes on the guards as they hunted over the ground below, hoping they'd stay on the path and not notice the slender gap between the trees that led to the meeting place, Much sensed Kate's fear. He watched helplessly as he saw one of the men knock his nearest colleague's shoulder and point towards the clearing entrance.

As two of the soldiers squashed into the space directly below them, Much heard the memory of Scarlet's voice booming in his ears. Will had been fuming with worry by the time they'd got back to the camp after saving Kate's father. "That girl should not have run towards you Much. I know she was scared, but if Gisburne saw…if he made the connection…" Scarlet hadn't been able to finish his sentence, but none of the others had argued with him, and when Much had looked to Robin for reassurance, he'd seen the same grave concern etched on his face.

As the soldiers searched the clearing below, Kate mumbled out of the corner of her mouth, 'what are they hunting for?'

'Me.' Much couldn't bring himself to say, 'us.'

Kate blanched. 'What!?'

'Ssshhh!'

Chastened by Much's concern and the close proximity of the Sheriff's men, Kate gulped, her shoulders trembling with fright at the prospect of being caught.

'But, the sack…' She pointed downwards, but daren't say more as Much had taken a firm hold of her arm. The soldiers were moving away.

It felt like forever between the soldiers leaving the meeting place and them eventually moving away. When Much spoke, his words rushed out in an exhalation of concern. 'They've gone. Did they find the sack?'

'I don't know. I can't believe they didn't look up. I'm glad you were 'olding my hand.'

'Was I? Oh, yes.'

Overcome with relief, Kate found herself giggling, but she wasn't sure what was funny. 'Didn't you notice?'

'No, I just wanted you safe… I don't have to let go now, do I?'

'Not unless you want to.'

'I'll keep 'olding it then.' He slipped an arm around Kate's shoulders, helping protect her from the sharp gusts that darted through the trees highest branches. 'You're shaking. Come on, come closer.'

Flicking her red plait to one side, Kate rested her head on Much's shoulder. 'I keep thinking about what they would have done if they'd found us.'

Much, who'd been thinking exactly the same thing said, 'don't dwell on it. They didn't.'

'I always feel safe when you're around.'

'Me too. When *you're* around, I mean.' Reluctantly, Much pulled away, 'we should get down though, in case they come back.'

'You don't think they will, do you?'

'I don't know, but we can't take the risk.' Much stared out across the forest, 'they've gone for now, but there may be others. I know it's been ages, but I'm sure Gisburne will still be cross about what happened when we rescued your father. He may 'ave sent out extra patrols now the snow has gone.'

'Why do you think they searched for us today? Do you think it's because the King's levy is being collected from the village this afternoon?'

'I don't know.' Deciding to tell Robin about the possible coincidence of them being hunted so close to tax collection day, Much felt increasingly troubled as he helped Kate down the tree.

The flash of relief Kate had experienced at the soldier's retreat dissolved into panic as she hit the forest floor. 'Much! The sack. It's gone.'

'You sure?'

Kate pointed to the trees at the back of the clearing. 'It was there. I stuffed it beneath some old autumn leaves before we climbed. Now it's gone.'

'What was in it?'

Her cheeks coloured as she said. 'I thought we might get cold, and there was nothing else to give this month. The winter has been harsh. It was just blankets in case we needed them.'

'Well they didn't see us, so that's good.' Much's mind raced, hoping that, if the soldiers had found the sack, they'd assume it belonged to someone living rough in the forest. He hadn't seen one of them carrying a sack as they'd walked away, but then he hadn't had the best view, and he'd been busy watching for the other three guards to join the search. 'I wish we did need them, but now I have to get you back.'

The panic Kate had been trying to keep to herself was all too clear now. 'You're not supposed to come to the village. What if you're seen?'

'Ts taking you back to safety. We'll go the back way, behind the barn. The soldiers know someone has been 'ere now, even though they don't know who. We can't come here again. Not ever.

'I'll carry the goodwill money. Best you don't have it on you until we's safe. Just in case.'

Kate gazed around, her face etched with sadness.

Understanding how difficult it would be for them not to return, Much hoped he sounded braver than he felt. 'Right, this is when you show me 'ow good you are at moving quiet. Remember everything I teached you.'

Kate nodded, but as she gave the meeting place one last look she whispered, 'Much, I'm scared.'

***

De Rainault's toadish stare was getting on Gisburne's nerves as he divided the coins into those that were marked and those which weren't.

'And?'

'Nearly all of money collected from Papplewick this afternoon has been marked by my dagger.' He snapped the box shut with a flourish. 'We have it, my lord. At last! Proof that the villagers have been receiving money from Robin Hood. I shall go and arrest them all now, then the outlaws are bound to come and...'

'No, Gisburne.' The Sheriff stared at the pile of marks. 'You will arrest them. All of them. The villagers and the outlaws - but not yet. We can't afford for this to fail. Get some wine. We are going to plan very carefully. This time the capture of Robin Hood and his outlaws is not going to go wrong.'

MARCH

CHAPTER 19

William despaired as Sir Guy of Gisburne and five soldiers cantered into Papplewick. Dusk had already fallen. It was a strange hour for the Sheriff's men to come so close to the edge of Sherwood. A sense of fear clutched at his chest. Automatically he looked around for Kate, hoping she was still busy in the hen house beside the barn, out of harm's way.

Stepping towards the unwanted visitors, William took a firmer grip of his staff. He knew he'd never use it to strike another human being, yet he felt better for having it.

'How can we help you, my lord?'

Gisburne glared down his haughty nose at the head villager. 'I never need help from scum like you!'

William said nothing, remembering what Edward of Wickham had told him about the advantages of acting like the simple serf Gisburne wanted him to be.

'Search the place!' No sooner had the order been issued, than the men-at-arms were throwing the villagers possessions around, kicking over barrels and making as much mess as they could.

'If you told me what you were looking for, perhaps I could save you some time, my lord.'

Gisburne glowered at William while the chaos continued around him. 'You will stay right where you are until I say otherwise.'

***

The vibration of the horse's hooves had alerted Kate to the soldiers' presence before she'd heard Gisburne's unmistakable voice.

Taking two steps towards her father, she then came to an abrupt halt in the middle of the chicken coop. Memories of the last time she'd seen Sir Guy of Gisburne up close stopped her in her tracks.

What if he remembers me as the girl who was dragged from the barn…what if he saw me almost run to Much and…

Crouching down, Kate whispered to the nearest chicken, 'I'm being foolish. Father has been free for ages. Why would Gisburne remember the likes of me? I'm less important to his kind that you are little hen.'

Trying to block out the noise of the deliberately heavy-handed search, hoping the hen house would be spared, Kate froze as the yell of a man screaming in pain hit her ears. She exhaled slowly, shutting her eyes as it was followed by a second agonised shout and then the pounding of eager booted feet.

Less than a minute later, a roar was unleashed from Gisburne's throat. 'Kate of Papplewick. If you don't show yourself now, I will do to your father what I did to David of Papplewick.'

For the briefest second Kate glanced at the path that would lead her away, out of Papplewick and deep into Sherwood. The path that led to Much.

'I said now, girl,' hissed Gisburne.

On shaky legs, Kate ran as fast as she could in the direction of the shouting. Not wanting to think what would happen when she got there, she looked anxiously at her father and the villagers who were milling around, uncertain what to do, before giving Gisburne a clumsy curtsey. 'Can I help you, my lord?'

'Men! Take her.'

'No, my lord. Please!' William's jowly face went deathly white as two soldiers grabbed his daughter, twisting her arms up behind her back. 'What's she done?'

Kate could feel the imprint of the fingers of the men on her arms. Although they both held her tight, the guard on her right was relishing his work far more than his colleague. She gasped in pain as he pressed his nails harder into her flesh.

'What has she done? Well that *is* an interesting question!' Gisburne unsheathed his sword, waving the tip menacingly close to William's throat. 'As if you didn't know.'

Dismounting from his horse, Gisburne drew nearer to Kate. He regarded her shrewdly, as if he was trying to work something out. 'I've seen you before.' Sir Guy swung his sword round to acknowledge the soldier who Kate feared was about to break her arm. 'My man here has learnt something very useful from one of your neighbours. I'm sure you heard how persuasive he can be.'

The cry from the barn. Kate's heart sank. Sensing what was coming next, she wanted to close her eyes, to escape the gloating face of the odious man in front of her and think of happier things. Times with her mother, with Much, with her father; anything, to deflect from the numbness that was surging up and down her arm and the triumph in Gisburne's eyes.

'We heard the cry, my lord.' William kept his voice steady, but Kate could see her father was afraid.

'Your daughter has been meeting with an outlaw in Sherwood. Robin Hood has been helping you just as we said he had.'

'No, my lord!'

'Do not trouble to deny it! I have proof and now I see this chit up close, I know which of Robin Hood's wretches she meets with.' Gisburne shook his blonde head at Kate in mock disappointment, 'Didn't the simpleton tell you not to run towards him in case I made the connection? Foolish girl. Clearly Hood is not training his helpers as well as he used to. You're as backwards as the boy.' With a finely tuned tut, Gisburne twisted on the spot and, without warning, swung the flat his sword with brutal speed. It smacked William across his left shoulder, which sent him stumbling along the grass. 'Take that as a warning. We'll be back for the girl.'

With a nod at his men, Kate was thrown to the ground and the soldiers remounted their horses. They were gone as fast as they'd appeared, leaving the villagers confused, disorientated and frightened.

'Daughter, are you alright?' William, leaning more heavily on his staff than before, came to where the soldiers had deposited Kate.

Trying to be brave, she brushed her muddy palms briskly down her skirts. 'Bit bruised, but I'll be alright.'

Gathering around them, the people of Papplewick were united in concern. Every individual was thinking back to the demise of their former head villager.

Knowing they were waiting for him to speak, William tore his eyes from his only child. 'Gisburne spoke of proof that the outlaws have helped us. We need to find out what that proof is, for I know that not one of you has given the Sheriff reason to question us. And although two of the outlaw's have been here in times of great need, great care was taken to conceal those visits.'

There was general agreement as Kate asked, 'who was the man in the barn, is he alright? Could someone look after him?'

William looked at her proudly before searching amongst the gathered crowd, noting a missing face. 'It must have been Simon who gave you away.'

'He had no choice. He'll feel guilty, as well as be in pain from whatever that horrid man did to him, but it wasn't Simon's fault. I shall go and tell him he's forgiven.'

Sending some people to help Kate with Gisburne's victim, William consulted with his friends. 'The Sheriff will send men to lie in wait for the outlaws.' Again there were murmurings of agreement. 'Therefore,' William pulled himself to his full height, banging his staff upon the churned up grass, 'the answer is clear. Neither Robin Hood, nor a single one of his followers, must come here. Ever again. No matter what the emergency.'

***

Back in Sherwood, Friar Tuck looked grave as he sat down at the camp fire with Robin. 'There are more rumours in Wickham that the Sheriff is gathering a force against the villages that help us.'

Robin gave a curt bob of his head. 'And they'll be saying the Sheriff has proof.'

'How did you know that?'

'Because we've had the evidence in our grasp for some time. Months even.' Robin was furious with himself. 'Why didn't I see it before? It's so simple.'

'Robin?'

'Arrogant fool that I am, I didn't believe Gisburne or the Sheriff capable of anything so clever. How wrong I was.'

'Are you going to tell me what you're talking about?'

Robin nodded, 'It'll be easier if I show you.'

'Of course.' Keeping his voice down as Robin picked up a small money bag, Tuck glanced around the camp, 'and where are John and Much?'

'Fishing.' Robin poured the contents of the bag onto the ground. 'Any other news from Wickham?'

'Apparently a silk merchant, one Reynard Felix will be on his way to Nottingham tomorrow. Quite a wealthy man of some repute.'

'Is he now?' Robin gave a slow smile. 'He sounds like a man we need to talk to.'

CHAPTER 20

The birds were in fine voice as Much edged towards the former meeting place. He paused, his hand on the hilt of his sword. Only once he was convinced the space was deserted, did he cross through its entrance.

Poking around, remembering what he could from Nasir's guidance on tracking people, Much investigated every scattered fragment of wood and blade of grass. His hand traced the line of the fallen tree trunk as he pictured himself sat there with Kate. He smiled.

Satisfied nobody had been there recently, Much backed out of the clearing and moved on through Sherwood. Continuing to be extra cautious, he travelled for another ten minutes before reaching the dip in the line of trees he'd been watching for.

Sliding between the closely placed oaks and hoping Kate remembered where he said to meet, he whispered her name.

'I'm here,' she replied. Determined to keep her fears about the future of Papplewick to herself, Kate rushed to Much's side and sank into his arms. 'I was getting worried. Are you alright?'

'I was checking the old place to make sure soldiers weren't waiting for us, but there's nobody there.'

With a critical eye, Much surveyed the tiny hollow. The tree branches knitted together overhead, letting only a few chinks of light in though their leaves. Although this meant it was cooler and darker than their previous hideout, it was also harder to locate from the outside.

'This is okay though, isn't it? Bit cramped maybe.'

'It's feels nice and safe.' Kate indicated a patch of ground at the foot of a thickly trunked oak. 'There's nothing to sit on, but we'd be quite comfortable down there maybe.'

Much grinned, 'umm… you don't have anything for me this time? No blankets or anything…'

'No I...' The shine in Kate's eyes dulled and then disappeared. To his horror, Much realised she was fighting the urge to cry.

'Whatever's wrong?'

As Much guided her to sit at the foot of the tree, Kate chocked out her words, scrubbing angrily at her weeping eyes. 'I'm not supposed to be here, but I knew you would be, so I had to come. I couldn't not! But father said I shouldn't.'

'Why? Is Papplewick in danger?'

'Yes, no...I don't know. Soon it might be.' Kate blew out a ragged breath. She knew she wasn't making sense. 'I told father about last time. I had to explain about the missing blankets and how you never got them and why.'

'Ah, yes.' Much recalled the outlaws horrified faces when he'd told them about the last goodwill meeting. 'I told Robin too. He didn't like it. I wondered if he'd stop me coming today.' Much paused, unhappy with what else he had to say. 'There are rumours that Gisburne's gathering a force against all the villages that help us. Tuck heard about it when he visited Wickham yesterday.'

Tears ran down Kate's face now, but she fought to keep herself composed. 'It's more than rumours. That's what I was going to tell you.'

'What's happened?'

With a sigh, Kate rolled up her sleeve. 'This for a start.'

The bruise was the size of a man's palm. Much had no trouble imagining how tightly Kate's arm had been pinched to produce the shocking purple and green patches that decorated her freckled skin.

Tight lipped, Much's face was ashen as Kate explained.

'One of Gisburne's men did it. They came last night. Grabbed my arm so forceful I thought it would snap. The villagers are frightened. One of them told Sir Guy I was messenger to the outlaws.'

'No! Kate, how could they!?' Frustrated anger welled in the pit of Much's stomach.

'They were afraid. Everyone is.' Kate's voice was weighed down with resignation. 'The soldiers said this was a warning. They said they'd be back for me.'

Furious, he leapt to his feet. 'How dare he, how...hang on...' Abruptly still, Much knelt next to Kate, his expression furrowed. 'Gisburne doesn't do warnings. Not anymore. Why didn't he take you away with him, or kill you right there? He's planning something.'

'Father says he's waiting for you and Robin to come and save me. He reckons Gisburne will lie in wait and trap you all. There are men stalking the village.'

'So how did you get out?'

Kate buried her head onto Much's shoulder. 'You taught me to be quiet and listen, remember.'

Pride in Kate threatened to overwhelm him as he stroked her hair. 'Yeah, I did! And you're really good at it.'

'Father wants to take me away from Papplewick. He has a sister in Derby. He wants to go there. When Father sees I'm gone he'll be furious.' Kate's voice became a reluctant murmur. 'We're leaving today.'

'Today?' For a second Much thought his heart had stopped beating. 'He can't take you away. Can he?'

'He doesn't want the soldiers to get me.'

Seized with emotions he didn't understand, Much walked in circles within the cramped space. 'This is my fault... if I hadn't come here and given you the money and...

Kate's plait waved from side to side as she shook her head. 'We would have all died from starvation or be in prison for not paying what we owe, or far worse.' She paused and looked Much in the eye. 'It's been a year. It's not like it's been six weeks.'

'I'll sort it out. I will. I promise. I'll go to Robin and...'

This time it was Kate who laid a finger on Much's lips. 'There's nothing you can do. If you and Robin and all your friends saved us, what then? What about the next time? Gisburne knows I've been meeting you. That only means one thing for me - or worse - for the whole village. None of you can come to Papplewick, not for a very long time.'

Much leaned forward, his voice eager, pleading Kate to agree with the solution he was sure she already knew he was about to offer. 'You could stay with us... Robin wouldn't mind and...'

'And what about my father?'

They sat in silence for a long time, listening to the arrhythmic rustle of the leaves above them.

Eventually Much said, 'Maybe you won't have to go. Maybe it'll be alright. I'll ask Herne to help and then we could stay together.'

Kate held Much's hand tighter. 'Maybe.'

'I...I've never had a friend like you before.'

'You could still be my friend.' Even though she knew what she was saying was hopeless, Kate kept talking. They both needed false hope, even if it was only something to cling onto for a little while. 'You could come to Derby when you aren't busy saving people.'

'Yeah. I could, couldn't I.'

More time passed, neither one letting go of the other, until Kate spoke the words they'd been avoiding. 'I should go. We need to leave for Derby before Gisburne does whatever he's planning.'

'Right.'

'Much?'

'Yeah.'

'Can we have one more cuddle first?'

***

'Is it done?'

'The exchange is made.' Nasir bowed his head. 'Papplewick is not as careful as it should be with valuables. They did not see me.'

Marion looked at Robin, 'are you sure we shouldn't tell Much.'

'I don't like keeping secrets from him, but if we tell him, he'll tell Kate. It's safer she and William don't know. The money he took today is safe, and now Nasir has swapped the old marked money for clean coins, they'll be okay.'

Scowling, Scarlet thrust his sword into the earth, 'I hate that we can't do anything. Gisburne should die for this.'

'I've explained,' Robin snapped, feeling every bit as frustrated as Scarlet did. 'If we do anything, Gisburne will be proved right. Doing nothing is the only way to keep everyone in Papplewick safe.'

'I still hate it!'

'So do I.' Robin's eyes fell on the depleted supply of money and changed the subject. 'There's a prosperous silk merchant due from Lincoln on his way to Nottingham market, isn't that what Edward of Wickham told you, Tuck?'

'He did.' The friar chuckled, 'one Reynard Felix is due to pass through the forest today so he can dine with the Sheriff tonight, before setting up his stall tomorrow. Reynard Felix indeed!'

Robin smiled. 'Well let's welcome this lucky fox to the shire while we wait for Much to get back from seeing Kate.'

'I used to love the stories of Reynard the Fox. My father told them to me when I was a child.' Marion gave Robin a shrewd stare. 'Does this merchant have a reputation for cruelty or greed?'

'No.' Robin winked, 'I promise we won't harm a hair of his bushy tail.'

Picking up her bow, Marion couldn't help but smile. 'What are you up to?'

As the outlaws made their way deeper into the forest, Will nudged John's arm, 'why they going on about lucky foxes?'

'No idea, lad,' John shrugged, 'probably some story rich families told their children.'

'Oh. That'll be why we ain't heard of no foxes called Reynard then.'

CHAPTER 21

Reynard Felix's success as a silk merchant provided him with the means of paying two well set men to guard both his wares and his life. No stranger to travelling through hazardous places, he'd instructed them to have their wits about them as they drove the cart through Sherwood Forest.

While Reynard had been prepared for, even part expecting, a volley of arrows to announce the approach of the infamous outlaw Robin Hood and his men, he had not foreseen the carriage grinding to a halt with a cry of, 'there's a fallen cleric in the road, my lord,' hailing from the driver's seat.

Pulling his hood up against the keen spring breeze, he stuck his head out of the window. Reynard saw the stricken man in the middle of the road. He was clutching his knee, his corpulent frame rolling on the dusty track in a most undignified manner.

'Help him up, but keep your weapons close. It could be a trap.'

***

As Tuck flailed, Scarlet grinned at Robin. 'Born to be a mummer or a minstrel that one. He should be on the stage. What a performance!'

They could hear Tuck's cries of pain. 'Ohhh, woe is me! I was set upon. A man of the cloth, set upon by knaves! God will curse them most mightily.'

'Keep watch.' Robin nodded to John, Scarlet and Marion, as he and Nasir, each carrying a treasure box, darted to the rear of the vehicle as soon as Reynard vacated his comfy seat to join his men in assisting Tuck.

Listening for the signal which would tell them the men were returning, Nasir opened his empty box so Robin could fill it with the contents of Reynard's coin chest. Then, Nasir quickly refilled the merchant's chest with the marked coins they'd carried from the camp.

As Tuck's overloud, 'thank you, thank you good men. God will surely have a special place for you reserved in Heaven,' rang in his ears, Robin made sure

Reynard's money chest was back precisely where he'd found it.

Tuck's moans of "the villains took my purse of funds. I hope the Devil rots their souls" accompanied the outlaws as they dived back into the forest in time to see the friar being solicitously guided to the side of the road, and reverently sat upon a conveniently placed rock.

'Don't overdo it Tuck!' Little John mumbled, but he couldn't help chuckle as he heard his friend assure his saviours that he'd be fine once he'd regained his breath.

'I'll pray for you my brothers.'

As Reynard and his men clambered back into the cart, the merchant's hood fell back from his sumptuous cloak. Marion gasped at the sheer redness of the man's mane of hair. 'Well if he wasn't named Reynard at birth, I can see why the name came his way.'

'Marion?' Will looked furtively from side to side, making sure that his comrades couldn't hear him, 'So, this Reynard the Fox, is it a children's story then, or what?'

***

'Thanks to Nasir, Papplewick's money is already safe for the next tax payment.' Robin counted out the untarnished money into five empty pouches. 'That just leaves Wickham and Calverton's coins to be swapped over, and gives us some spare for emergencies. I don't want a single damaged piece going anywhere near the people of Sherwood; at least, not from our hands.'

Scarlet frowned, 'some will already be in circulation. It will have been spent at the markets.'

'As long as it doesn't appear in any future tax money for the Sheriff, then the villages should be safe. I know we can't do anything about the proof the Sheriff already thinks he has, but a letter to the treasury accusing De Rainault of defrauding the king might take his mind off our people for a while.'

'King's only person the Sheriff's more scared of then you Robin.' Tuck tied the pouches closed. 'I'll take Edward the clean money for Wickham now. Sooner the unmarked coins are in place, the better.'

Little John picked up one of the money bags, and weighed in his palm. Since his fishing conversations with Much, he'd been feeling his own lack of companionship keenly. 'Tell you what Tuck, why don't you take some replacement coins to Calverton? I'll take one to Wickham.'

The friar winked. 'Give our love to Meg, won't you?'

***

Robert de Rainault took a salacious pleasure in watching his steward serve the silk merchant the claret he'd found so bitter, while he kept to his own wine. He'd considered sending the whole barrel of unpleasant liquor to his brother, Abbot Hugo, but perhaps it was better to use it up on men who believed themselves better than they were, rather than sending it somewhere where there was a danger he'd end up having to drink it himself.

'Have you decided upon your silks, my lord?' Reynard gestured to the four different rolls of material the Sheriff had instructed his steward to display upon the nearest table.

'The dark blue I think. Two rolls.'

Reynard waved a hand towards one of his men, who swiftly collected up the unwanted goods and left the hall. 'You have good taste, my lord Sheriff. A fine shade, close to the royal purple, but not so close as to cause offence to his majesty.'

Only the influence his guest had in the Kings' court sealed De Rainault's lips from the cutting barb he would otherwise thrown in the salesman's direction after such a comment. 'It's fine cloth. I'm glad you got it here safely.'

Wincing as he took a draft of the claret, Reynard politely put the goblet down, saying nothing of the sour taste. 'I confess I was on the alert throughout Sherwood. We hear the tales of Robin Hood even in the markets of France and Spain, but the worst we encountered was a fallen cleric who needed our aid.'

'A cleric?' The Sheriff's eyes narrowed. 'No harm had come to him I trust?'

'He described two knaves assaulting him for his money pouch. We helped him to the side of the road. I offered him a lift to Nottingham, but he declined. No great harm had come to him I think, but for wounded pride.'

'This cleric,' De Rainault asked, 'not a young man, if he couldn't get to the side of the road unaided?'

'No great age,' Felix grunted, 'but he was not built for flight. We clearly over feed our men of God, my lord.'

Thoughtful, the Sheriff said, 'But at least you met no outlaws along the way.'

'I'll drink to that!' The merchant raised his goblet to do just that, before remembering the taste of the contents and putting it down again.

'Gisburne!' The Sheriff called across the length of the great hall to where his deputy had been sullenly chewing on a chicken leg. 'Fetch the payment for Master Felix.'

On Gisburne's return, a bag of coins in his hand, Reynard bowed graciously, 'and while I'm here, my lord Sheriff, 'I will pay what I owe for tomorrow's market fee. So much more gentlemanly than paying your collectors like a common trader.'

The Sheriff and his deputy looked at each other with equally raised eyebrows at the men's sense of self importance, as Reynard opened his money box and counted his pitch fee onto the table.

***

'She's gone.' It had taken a large mug of ale and a great deal of persuasion to get Much to break the silence he'd clung to since his return from Papplewick several hours before. 'At least she will be by now.'

'Gone?' Robin frowned, wondering if he should have told Much about swapping the marked money for clean money after all, and so removing Gisburne's proof that the outlaws were continuing to provide the village with tax money.

'Gisburne's men tortured one of the villagers. He gave Kate away. Told Sir Guy that Kate meets me every month.'

Robin closed his eyes and again cursed his slowness at working out what Gisburne had been up to. It didn't matter that the proof of collusion was gone, if Kate's role as messenger to the outlaws was revealed, her life was in danger and she was wise to leave. They may have saved the village future rancour without having to fight Gisburne in the process, but they couldn't save Much from a broken heart.

'I'm so sorry, Much.'

The youngest outlaw stared into the fire. He was quiet for a while before he turned back to Robin. 'When we was speaking to 'Arold, he mentioned that the real tax money was going a new way, and then he mumbled on a bit about stuff cos he was drunk.'

'Go on, Much.' Robin gave an encouraging smile.

'I reckon I needs to be very busy for a while, and I thinks that Gisburne and the Sheriff have had their way far too much this past year.'

'I can't argue with that.'

'He kept saying taxes were going to be mocking 'em didn't he?' Much shifted against the hard ground. 'What if that isn't what he was saying? What if he meant the taxes were going to be going via Rockingham? I know it's sort of the wrong way for London, but what if that's what's 'appening cos it would keep the money further away from us, and what if we wents along the road that leads that way there and waited for 'em?'

'Much,' Robin leapt to his feet, pulling his friend up after him, 'I have no idea what we'd do without you.'

'Do you think I'm right, Robin?'

'I do.' Robin gestured across to where the others were chatting under the trees. 'Why don't you go and tell them your plan to get our people's money back?'

'Me?' Much stood a little taller. 'Do you think my plan might work?'

'Of course I do.' Robin gave him an encouraging smile. 'You're a man now, Much.'

***

The Sheriff threw the coins across the hall, aiming them at Gisburne's head. 'Look! Look what that sly fox paid me with.'

Gisburne frowned as he shielded his face from a pelting of marks. 'How can that be? No villager could afford Felix's silks?'

Holding up a coin, feeling the unmistakable grove made by his deputy, De Rainault threw it into the fire. 'And yet every coin he gave me bears your carving! Every... single... one. And if he has them, anyone could have them, and our proof is gone!'

'I tell you it's impossible, my lord.' Gisburne's face had taken on a waxy hue as he backed away from his outraged master. 'God alone knows how Felix got hold of those coins but...'

De Rainault stopped moving. 'God does know.'

'What?'

'The fallen cleric, Gisburne! The fallen cleric...' The Sheriff's words disappeared into a speechless hiss, which nonetheless found a way to rebound around the hall, until it suddenly crescendo-ed into a red faced shout. 'Months! Months of waiting, of plotting! Why do I ever believe your plans will work Gisburne!?'

APRIL

CHAPTER 22

Rain bounced off Much's hood and shoulders as he trudged through the forest. He wasn't sure why he was going there. It was pointless. She wouldn't be there.

Word had come to the outlaws the day after he'd seen last Kate. Papplewick was once again in need of a new head family. No one who already lived there wanted the position, although Robin had said that would make no difference in the end. If a new family didn't come in, then one of the exiting elders would have the position thrust upon him the next time Gisburne or the Sheriff arrived in Papplewick.

It was raining like this the first time I met her.

Much kept his right hand inside his cloak. It rested on his dagger as he edged forward, doing his best to avoid the worst of the puddles that dotted the widening path.

He'd felt reassured for the future of Papplewick when his friends had explained about the Sheriff's plan to prove the outlaw's were helping the villagers. And he'd almost understood Robin when he'd explained about the marked money Gisburne had ensured the outlaws stole. Money that was now largely in the possession of a merchant on his way to London, as well as being spent, quite innocently, all over the shire, leaving the Sheriff to explain to the Treasury why so many clipped coins were reaching them from Nottingham.

But it had been too late for Kate and her father.

Even Much's triumph at leading the outlaws to capture the real tax money, rather than the Sheriff's decoy money, from the road to Rockingham, had only cheered him for a while.

He could hear Robin's voice rattle around his head as he stepped over a fallen branch. "You'll get over it, Much. Kate had to leave, Much. It's not your fault, Much. Be happy she's safe, Much…"

Kicking a stone into the trees, Much muttered into the downpour. 'It's alright for you Robin, you've got Marion. My Kate's miles away and all you can say is, "you're a man now, Much. It happens, Much."'

Sighing, he pulled his hood lower over his face as he reached the entrance to their original meeting place. He wasn't sure why he'd headed there, rather than to the new one. He'd told himself he needed to see it one more time. To say goodbye to it properly. Maybe then he'd accept that Kate had truly gone.

'At least she's safe.' Much spoke the words to the trees bracingly, hoping that saying them aloud would make him feel better. Derby wasn't that far away, and Little John knew the way if he decided to go and find her.

The fallen trunk was still there. Much sat down, keeping his arms wrapped around his knees, the rainwater dripping with light rhythmic splashes all around him. Closing his eyes, he spoke into the empty space.

'I know you can't hear me Kate, but I wish you could. I'm in our special place. There's no soldiers about. After you and your father had gone, we went to the road between Nottingham and Papplewick and stopped the soldiers before they got anywhere near the village. Robin said we should give the Sheriff something else to think about, so we set them running after us into the forest. They never got us of course cos...' Much found his throat closing in on his words, as he whispered, '...cos we is quiet and we listen.'

With an effort, he got back to his feet. 'Anyway, just thought you'd want to know that the Sheriff's bored with chasing villagers now. Robin's got him all worried that King John will be after him for defacing the royal coinage or something.' Much unexpectedly found himself smiling, 'Gisburne's been sent on an errand to London to sort things out, so it's quiet here for now. I might even come to Derby... just to say hello.'

He sighed, knowing in his heart that he wouldn't be setting a single foot towards Derby. 'I'd better get back. Little John was looking at me all worried earlier. I just wanted you to know that... well... you know. You do know... I's sure you know... so bye then, Kate.'

Turning towards the path, Much froze. A feeling that he couldn't explain, but was sensible enough not to ignore, was rising rapidly, making his spine tingle. Something wasn't right. He swivelled on the spot; pulling his dagger as he crept to the far edge of the clearing. Kneeling, Much could see a grey shape buried in a heap of rotting leaves banked up behind the hollow. It was a sack.

'A sack of apples?' Much laughed. 'Ha! What else have you left me? I wonder if...'

'Much?'

The sound was so weak, he almost missed it.

'Kate!' He could just see her, half buried in the leaves beyond the sack, with only her face and one hand on show. 'Oh, what's wrong?'

Her voice struggled to form the words, as she mouthed, 'I came back, Much… I came…'

A distraught Much came to her side. He could see the shiny pallor of her face as he knelt next to her. He couldn't imagine how long it had taken her to walk here from Derby alone, carrying a sack of apples. 'No, no. You're bleeding! What happened?'

The word 'soldiers' formed on her dry cracked lips.

'No!' Much looked helplessly from side to side, but there was no one there. No danger remained, but there was no one to call for help either.

Shivering against her leaf blanket, Kate murmured, 'I wanted… I needed… I'm cold.'

'Shhh! I'll warm you.' He lifted Kate so he could cradle her on his lap. He saw the wound then. It had been a knife, and it had gone deep into her side. Her tunic and cloak were caked with blood.

He tried to swell the panic that was rising in him. 'Hold me, Much.'

'I am. Kate, you're hurt bad. I don't think I can…'

'I know.' She licked her lips. 'They was waiting, I couldn't…it was too quick.'

Unsure how he was speaking past the lump in his throat, Much stroked her hair while finally counting the freckles on her nose he'd speculated about so often over the past twelve months.

'It's alright,' he said, but his words felt empty. 'We'll stay here forever. You and me, like this, in our special place.'

'Much, I…'

'I know, Kate. I do too. It's okay.' He watched as her eyes flickered closed, pleading with Herne to help him keep a smile on his face. He desperately didn't want her to see the tears forming in his eyes and tried to squeeze them away. 'Listen to the birds. They're singing for us.'

As they listened to the spring chorus, Much's voice fractured. 'See, they's singing just for us, Kate.'

He didn't know how long he held her before he felt her body grow heavy in his arms and then relax. Pulling her closer, Much watched as the pain across her face faded into serenity.

'Kate? My Kate…'

EPILOGUE

Little John had led the way.

His knowledge of the roads to Derbyshire, well remembered from his life in the county long before his outlawry, guided them on the slow painful journey from Sherwood.

No one had bothered the party of six men and one woman with the litter carrying the carefully wrapped body. Neither villager nor guard crossed their path. Much half hoped they would. Any excuse to hurry as many of the Sheriff of Nottingham's men to Hell as he could, would have been welcome.

Will Scarlet, trapped in the personal remembrances Kate's death had sent to the forefront of his mind, had been particularly quiet. Yet the words he hadn't spoken had reached Much in a look of understanding, and he'd been glad of them.

After they'd collected Kate from where Much had left her, reverently covered in his cloak to keep off the worst of the relentless rain, Marion had taken him to one side. Shooing away the men to find a cart in which to transport Kate to her father, she'd placed her shivering friend by the fire. Giving him some stew, which remained un-eaten, Marion had covered Much's shoulders in sheepskin to warm him from the triple assailants of shock, grief and rain soaked clothing.

She hadn't asked any questions. Not one. But she'd found herself listening anyway: Much talked for ages about everything Kate had done, everything she'd meant. Her laugh, her keenness to learn to move quietly and to listen. And that she'd had fifteen light brown freckles dotting her nose.

'Five on the left, six on the right and four in the middle.'

On arrival in Derby, Friar Tuck had begged them shelter in a cooper's barn. Robin, Marion and Little John had gone in search of William of Papplewick and his sister, while Scarlet, Tuck and Nasir stood on reverential guard over their fallen messenger.

Much had stayed with Kate. Not moving from his vigil until her father came. He'd been proud of how he'd kept his emotions in check on the journey, but as William of Papplewick entered the barn, leaning heavily on his staff, his face looking as if it had aged twenty years in a month, Much's strength deserted him.

A taciturn Little John watched his young friend with solicitous care as William ran a single finger across the litter. 'My child.'

Half afraid William would turn his grief on him, and half hoping he would, for Much felt he deserved it for even daring to become friends with someone so special, when just speaking to him could put her in danger, the young outlaw found himself engulfed in a most unexpected hug.

'You loved her too. I'm glad she knew love, I just wish…' Neither William of Papplewick nor Much the Miller's Son had been able to speak for some time after that.

***

Their progress home was slow but purposeful.

Whatever had happened, however torn apart Much felt inside, he knew the people of Wickham, Calverton, Papplewick and all the other settlements subject to the whims of England's harsh laws, would need them just as they always had.

Much noticed Scarlet walking nearby and felt the weight of guilt lay heavy on his honest shoulders. 'I'm sorry Will. I didn't mean it, you know, when I threatened you with my knife that time, I…'

Scarlet gave Much a self-conscious pat on the shoulder. 'I'd have done the same.'

'Would you?'

'Well no, I'd have killed ya, but I'd have wished I hadn't afterwards.'

***

Two more hours of steady walking passed with barely a word spoken, before Robin spotted Sherwood on the horizon.

As the welcoming embrace of the forest came within reach, Nasir fell into step with Much.

'Love is a gift. You do not feel lucky, but you are. Use what Kate gave you.'

'Gave me?'

'Anger, strength and compassion.' Nasir's countenance was solemn as he spoke rare words of sober comfort, 'you had all three before; but now you understand what they truly mean.'

122

Touched by the Saracen's sentiment, Much inclined his head as he gazed ahead towards the trees.

'Kate helped me to remember a promise I made. A promise I's not allowed myself to think about for a very long time. That I'd worked so hard *not* to think about I'd almost forgotten I'd ever made it; although...' Much gulped as he added, '...I'll never forget why or how it was made.'

On hearing Much, Robin Hood stopped walking.

His eyes were far away, following a line that his arm was tracing as he pointed towards the soul of Sherwood Forest.

Remembering a life he'd never lived, Robert of Huntingdon then spoke with a voice that was not his own, but might have been.

A voice that would last for now, for then and for always.

'Nothing's forgotten, Much. Nothing is *ever* forgotten.'

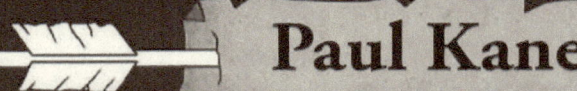

www.ingramcontent.com/pod-product-compliance
Lightning Source LLC
Chambersburg PA
CBHW020144180626
46810CB00004B/1727